GEORGES DE LYS

PENTHESILEA

TRANSLATED AND WITH AN INTRODUCTION BY

BRIAN STABLEFORD

THIS IS A SNUGGLY BOOK

ISBN: 978-1-64525-072-2

GEORGES DE LYS (1855-1931) was the pseudonym of Georges Fontaine de Bonnerive. He was in service when he published all of his early work, which included three poetry collections, beginning with *Les Idoles* (1884) and one naturalistic novel, *Raymond Meyreuil* (1886), before he published *Une Idyll à Sedôm* (1889). He went on to publish *Penthesilea* (1896), and numerous other novels, volumes of poetry and military studies, but little attention has been paid to him by orthodox literary historians, perhaps partly because the violent eroticism of the *Une Idyll à Sedôm* cast a shadow over his reputation from which it never entirely recovered, in spite of two of his subsequent works being awarded prizes by the Académie française.

BRIAN STABLEFORD'S scholarly work includes *New Atlantis: A Narrative History of Scientific Romance* (Wildside Press, 2016), *The Plurality of Imaginary Worlds: The Evolution of French roman scientifique* (Black Coat Press, 2017) and *Tales of Enchantment and Disenchantment: A History of Faerie* (Black Coat Press, 2019). In support of the latter projects he has translated more than a hundred volumes of *roman scientifique* and more than twenty volumes of *contes de fées* into English.

Contents

Introduction

"PENTHÉSILÉE" by Georges de Lys (Georges Fontaine de Bonnerive, 1855-1931), here translated as *Penthesilea*, was initially published in two parts in the 15 March and 1 April 1896 issues of *La Nouvelle Revue*. It was the author's second major contribution to the subgenre of neo-Romantic accounts of *moeurs antiques* [ancient mores], following *Une Idylle à Sedôm* (1889; tr. as *An Idyll in Sodom*). It was published in the same year as Pierre Louÿs' *Aphrodite, moeurs antiques*, which became the best-selling novel of the 1890s in France and launched a bandwagon on which many other writers promptly leapt, but it must have been planned and written in ignorance of that imminent development in the marketplace. Whereas the earlier venture had been based on the Bible, "Penthesilée" referred back to a different species of "holy writ": the "Homeric tradition," ultimately to the document most likely to appeal to a serving soldier like Fontaine de Bonnerive, the *Iliad*, although it draws its immediate inspiration from some of the many "sequels" to Homer's epic produced in Classical times and subsequently transfigured on multiple occasions by various hands.

The "original" version of the story of Penthesilea is attributed to *Aethiopis*, an epic alleged to have been composed in the eighth century B.C. by one Arctinus of Miletus. Not written down, in an era before the widespread use of the Greek alphabet, the contents of the work are only known via second-hand summaries and recyclings. *Aethiopis* recounts that Penthesilea came to assist the Trojans in their struggle against the Greeks, accompanied by twelve warrior women. At the end of a day-long battle, she confronted Achilles, who killed her, but after removing her helmet to reveal her face he fell in love with her. Rebuked for his weakness by Thersites, Achilles killed him too, and then had to go to Lesbos in order to be ritually purified before returning to Troy to continue the fight.

Variant versions of Penthesilea's story apparently existed, similarly known only through brief second-hand accounts, in some of which she was on the other side, Priam having previously made war on the Amazons, but it was the *Aethiopis* story that became canonical within the Homeric tradition, and that version is fugitively and subtly echoed in Virgil's *Aeneid* (first century B.C.), where Penthesilea becomes a tragic figure leading an entire army. Images presumed to represent Achilles carrying the dying or dead Penthesilea cropped up frequently in Greek and Roman art before then, an apparent subject of specialization by one painter in the fifth century B.C. employed in a workshop that mass-produced vases. In the fourth century A.D., the poet Quintus Smyrnaeus embroidered and transfigured the story of Penthesilea again in his *Posthomerica*, relating that Penthesilea went to Troy motivated by grief after killing her sister Hippolyta in a hunting accident, intent on dying in battle—an ambition she fulfilled, along with several of her comrades, but in so doing inspired the Trojan women, who were watching from the walls, to join the war.

The story of Penthesilea was recycled in the Renaissance by Boccaccio; he too has

Penthesilea slain in battle, using her story to argue the controversial case that men and women are potentially equal in strength and courage, and that it is only their upbringing that creates observed gender differences. That argument is carried forward obliquely in Georges de Lys' version of the story—which employs dramatic license to transfigure the story more drastically than his predecessors—but arrives at a markedly different conclusion there. More immediate successors of Boccaccio within the French tradition of chivalric Romance recruited Penthesilea to a group of valiant warrior women featured in verse and prose romances, her death routinely represented as a tragedy—a tragedy played out in reality when Jeanne d'Arc modeled herself on the female warriors of Romance in the course of the Hundred Years War and achieved mythical status in her own right. Such images bore further fruit in new sequels to the *Iliad*; Georges de Lys was evidently familiar with one of them, penned in the early seventeenth century by François Du Souhait, from which his own text borrows a passage improvised by Du Souhait from *Posthomerica*.

The most notable nineteenth-century precursor of George de Lys' version of the story was Heinrich von Kleist's drama *Penthesilea* (1808), in which it is Penthesilea who kills Achilles rather than *vice versa*, and is then stricken by mortal grief. Goethe considered the play to be unstageable, but it eventually became the basis of two operas, one by Othmar Schoeck (1927) and the other by Pascal Dusapin (2015). Saturated with Germanic *sturm und drang*, Kleist's version of the story exhibits a hyper-Romanticism with which the similarly-inclined Georges de Lys must have sympathized. Having no Cassandra to aid him, he could not know, of course, that Penthesilea would become a common reference-point in the writings of various twentieth-century feminists, or that she would provide the some-what ironic inspiration for the naming of the heroine of George Lucas' *Star Wars* (1977). When his *Penthesilea* appeared in the *Nouvelle Revue* the periodical was still owned by Juliette Adam, who had a considerable reputation as a pioneering feminist, but she no longer had any direct involvement in its editing, and her opinion of it, if she ever read it, is unrecorded.

Georges de Lys' version of Penthesilea's story departs radically from earlier versions in its conclusion, which brings the story firmly into line with the classic formula of Greek tragedy, as a strident exemplar of hubris demolished by Nemesis. The hubris in question is not so much the Amazon queen's personal arrogance—which falters more than once—but that of her imaginary race, and it is punished in a uniquely striking manner, which gives the novella a remarkably dark and trenchant cutting edge. It is a conclusion of which few feminists would be likely to approve, in spite of its evident qualification as just desserts, but it has a force and pertinence that few could dispute.

As pastiche Greek tragedies go, *Penthseilée* is as pure as it is relentless. No less flamboyant than *Une Idylle à Sedôm*, it is significantly crueler—no easy achievement in juxtaposition with a Biblical fantasy whose climax is a rain of divine fire that consumes the innocent as well as the guilty with a remarkable lack of discrimination. The author's other works seem mild by comparison, and the early influence he had taken from the Decadent Movement ebbed away after the turn of the century, when he was no longer in military service. *Penthesilée*, however, remains an impressive work, remarkable in its uncompromising excess, fully deserving rescue from the oblivion into which it inevitably fell, hidden in the pages of a periodical and never before published in book form.

❋

The translation was made from the volume of the *La Nouvelle Revue* including the relevant issues, which is reproduced on the Bibliothèque Nationale's *gallica* website.

—Brian Stableford, April 2020

PENTHESILEA

I
For the Crown

THE time had come to enter into campaign, to know men, not by means of an enervating sojourn among allied peoples, but by the more glorious capture of enemies, whose handsome warriors, before being sacrificed to the Sun, would assure the posterity of the noble Amazons by means of their ephemeral union.

And those same men, the men that they would have held in their arms, who would have slept on their bosoms, would also affirm, by their inexorable torture, the scorn of the warrior women for the accursed sex.

The last expedition had been sterile. Of the three hundred and seventy young men selected from among the prisoners of war for their strength and their beauty, only a hundred and three daughters had been born. More numerous were the sons destined to rejoin among the shades the manes of their fathers, immolated after the engenderment.

One captive was still in the palace of the queen. The young Penthesilea had reserved him, so the people believed, in order to heighten with his torture the ritual ceremony of the weaning of the daughters, their consecration to the Sun, and the hecatomb of the new-born males, because she was irritated in the pride of her flesh and the revolt of her blood by having known the man without becoming a mother by that means.

And the impatient youth of the nation demanded the signal of the sovereign in order to rush to battles and joys.

Thus, a great acclamation filled Themiscrya[1] when, dusty and breathless, a foreign courier knocked on the gates of the city and responded to the interrogation of the guards:

1 Themiscrya, at the mouth of the Thermodon, on the southern coast of the Black Sea, is named by Herodotus as the capital of the Amazons.

"My name is Pheon of Ilios; I am the bearer of a message from my master, the venerable Priam, for your queen."

The people were not unaware of the assaults that were unfurling against the walls of Pergame[1] like tempestuous waves against an immobile reef. They knew the names of Agamemnon, chief of nations, the two Ajaxes, Nestor the wise, and Menelaus, the unconsolable husband. They had heard tales of the prudence of Ulysses, the splendor of Diomedes and the indomitability of Achilles. The coming of the messenger meant war; Priam was requesting the help of the invincible Amazons. And the crowd rejoiced in the imminent battles, evoking the vision of the enemies who would soon be their captives, their husbands and their victims: the Achaeans, the most handsome of men.

The messenger headed toward the queen's palace, escorted triumphally by the multitude.

---

1 Pergame is the French form of Pergamon, the name of an ancient Greek city that was briefly mistaken for Troy in one version of the story of Achilles, although quite different. The use of the term *Pergama* with reference to Troy itself was an eccentricity of the *Aeneid*, deriving from the fact that the literal meaning of *pergama* is "citadel." Like Virgil, Lys uses the Roman versions of the names of the gods and heroes associated with the Trojan war.

On the step of the throne the Trojan bowed and raised toward the queen the olive branch that made his person sacred. At a sign, he advanced, knelt down, rummaged in the bag suspended around his neck, and held out his master's message.

Penthesilea unrolled the papyrus and her forehead was darkened by a cloud.

"Go to your rest," she said, after a silence, "I will respond to your king's request tomorrow."

Hippolyta,[1] the queen's sister, standing beside her, had read the appeal addressed by the sovereign of Ilios to Penthesilea. That temporization revolted her. She enveloped his sister with a scornful gaze.

Coward, she thought.

---

1 Hippolyta is an Amazon queen featured in mythical accounts of Hercules and Theseus that are incompatible with accounts of Penthesilea, but which credit her with the same parentage, which is why Quintus Smyrnaeus made the two of them sisters in his revisionist *Posthomerica*, which invented the story of the fatal hunt embroidered and transformed by Lys for his own purposes. In some versions of the story of Theseus Hippolyta falls in love with the hero and marries him prior to his marriage to Phaedra, a motif apparently borrowed by Lys for redeployment and transfiguration in his own story.

In the depths of the royal gynaeceum, softly illuminated by clay lamps suspended by golden chains, on a snowy mass of silky fleeces, the divine Penthesilea, her youthful arms knotted around his neck, drew to her breast the charming head of Atys, the handsome captive. Her sea-blue irises were aimed amorously at the radiance of fluid gold in which the pupils of her lover swam. But her grip relaxed; a shadow darkened the pure forehead of the queen and anxiety spoiled the smile of her flowery mouth.

Disdainful of the laws, perjurer of the oaths of her race, the young queen had surrendered her heart to the captive; she was the servant of amour. First, anger had risen within her at the revelation of her weakness; she had fought against that enveloping cowardice, which further increased the shameful sterility of her marriage; but that revolt had foundered in the sensualities that her lover's kiss poured into her mouth.

When the day prescribed by the rites dawned, when the holocaust of the captives was imposed, her passion had invented the stratagem that conserved her joys. She consecrated her husband as the sacrifice due to the gods before the future expedition, as a special victim. The epoch having been distanced, the present joy had seemed to delay the fatal reckoning for such a long time . . . but now the time had elapsed.

Atys, her beautiful Atys! The murderous knife would bite into his neck, as white as a swan's, the blood would splash his face and glue the silken waves of his hair, so soft to the touch. His eyes, celestial mirrors of his life and his beauty, would be extinguished. His lips would close to words of love, and the horrifying vision would populate the insomnias of her henceforth-solitary nights.

The terror of that invocation had convulsed Penthesilea's young face. Atys contemplated it, his soul oppressed by his lover's anguish.

"What Fury is agitating your heart, Penthesilea? Close your ears to the Eumenide and heed my voice."

She burst forth, wildly: "Accursed be the day when a god knew my mother! Accursed be the sun that shone over my birth. Alas, I dare not blaspheme the hour that enabled me to know you . . . and yet, of that divine hour our misfortune was born. I am a queen, Atys; to be a queen is to be the slave of one's people; my subjects demand war, and the entry into campaign must be preceded by your death!"

"I know the rites of your race," declared Atys, valiantly. "What does it matter? Thanks to you, I have completed my life. Don't hesitate; order the altar to be elevated. I shall carry my head there glorified by your kisses."

"Have you understood my love so poorly that you believe that Penthesilea will be alive when Atys is dead? You alone are my life and my realm." And, throwing a warrior garment to the stupefied young Achaean, she said: "Take these garments and these weapons. My two best chargers are waiting for us. Before daylight we will have crossed the frontier. Hurry up, the hour is menacing."

"Penthesilea, I would be unworthy of you if I listened to your words. I will not let your glory wither. Obey your gods and satisfy your people."

"My glory? I don't care about it! My people? I hate them!" cried Penthesilea. "I want to live, and you are my life."

Atys admired the warrior woman. Then the joy of possessing her appeared to him, of growing old beside her at a familial hearth in the land of his ancestors. His love would be great enough to repay the beloved for the sacrifice of her homeland and her crown.

His courage weakened.

"You wish it . . . ?" he murmured.

She stifled the murmur with an embrace. "Finally!"

She tore off his clothing, and dressed him again in the costume of the Amazons. Already she was dragging him away, parting the curtains of the border . . .

A glint cut through the darkness. Without a cry, Atys collapsed; his large eyes were extinguished. On the threshold stood Hippolyta, her arms dangling, her hand clenching a dagger from which blood was dripping.

Penthesilea recoiled, white with despair; then, roaring, she bounded forward, her ax raised. Hippolyta dropped her dagger, folded her arms over her breast, and waited, holding her head high, and saying in a calm voice:

"I have saved the queen!"

II
The Amazons

PENTHESILEA was immobilized, her ax lowered, tamed by her sister's attitude. Hippolyta, assured of her triumph, drew the dejected queen away. She gave a brief order and the cadaver of Atys disappeared in the arms of slaves mutilated in the tongue and the sex. Penthesilea yielded, grim but vanquished.

Hippolyta evoked the benedictions with which the people would acclaim her, and imminent visions of glory. She foresaw the campaign, the magnificent welcome of Priam, the triumphant clamors of the skirmishes in which Penthesilea would combat Achilles, in which woman would vanquish man through her, and immolate the hero who had vanquished Hector.

The queen bowed her head, and Hippolyta spoke.

She spoke about the beauty of Argians[1] as blond as the sun god; she praised Helen and the women of that race for their divine grace. Among them they would capture new males, whose blood would embellish the daughters of the Amazons.

She spoke, still addressing the impassive queen. Suddenly, Penthesilea's rigid arm made an abrupt gesture, but Hippolyta had already retained it.

"You want to die?" she said, snatching away her dagger. "Lead your warriors into battle, then. Show them how a queen falls. Let your death at least be fecund. But if your soul is cowardly to the point of belying your blood and your dignity, if man has degraded you to the point that you prefer suicide to glorious death and the example that you can give to your people in the hour of battle, I will return your dagger to you—die! But after you, I will be queen, and know that your body, instead of burning on the royal pyre of a warrior will be thrown by my order to feed the jackals and the vultures. Your crime will be revealed, your

---

1 Lys appears to use "Argians" henceforth as a synomym for "Greeks," much as Homer used "Achaeans"—an example he was presumably following in the previous chapter in referring to Atys as an Achaean.

name stigmatized forever; mothers will relate your ignominy to their daughters, and to their daughters' daughters."

The queen stared at her sister; Hippolyta's eyes were already illuminated by proud sovereignty. Then she straightened up, imperiously.

"Go away! Tomorrow you will know my orders and my will."

At dawn, Penthesilea summoned her warriors, decreed the weaning of daughters born of the latest marriage and the solemn holocaust of the male children, in order to obtain celestial fervor and accomplish the rites.

She selected, for the messengers of her orders, the twelve companions who had rendered their valor and their grace dear to her. They were the blonde Clonie;[1] Polemusa, the singer of battle hymns; Deiona, skillful at anticipating the flight of birds with her arrows; Evadre, the tamer of restive stallions;

_____

1 This name is rendered Cléonie at this point in the *Nouvelle Revue* text, but the name is subsequently rendered as Clonie, in common with other accounts of the companions of Penthesilea enumerated in *Aethiopis* and cited by many recyclers of the story.

Autandre, expert in the training of blood-hounds; Bremusa the diviner; Hyppothoa, who surpassed the suppleness of trout in the waters of the Thermodon; Alcibia of the strong arm, whose darts transpierced the thickest bucklers; Antrobota, whose fawns had no equal in running; Derimarque, whose voice dominated the tumult of battles; Harmothoa, the most beautiful; and Thermodusa, the best at handling a spear.

The twelve messengers departed on their rapid horses, radiating from Themiscrya throughout Pontus, and the royal order transmitted by their mouths, divulged to the clamor of trumpets, carried from place to place, signaled by nocturnal fires lit on the summits of hills, assembled the subjects on the eve of the festival around the capital, while the pyre was built in the square of the sacred ceremonies.

Caravans extended along the roads filed toward the city, swelling at the crossroads, like the affluence of streams creating a river. Each young mother balanced on her shoulder, like a quiver, the leather sheath holding her child. From time to time, invoked by a tearful cry, one of them brought the nursling to her unique nipple in order to feed. The rare women who were proud of a double fruit suspended them alternately over the hip and the breast, amused by the gluttonous impatience of the one weaned of her place because there was only one at the feast.

Some were riding astride the hides of wild beasts, to which their weapons were secured. Others were making their way on foot, their baggage transported on carts hitched to aurochs and consigned to the guard of the elderly.

The infecund warriors had donned the tight tunic of combat, fabricated from the spotted skins of panthers and lynxes, like flowery fabrics. The sash that knotted it at the waist supported the quiver suspended over the left thigh. The legs were molded in breeches that were encased at the bottom by shoes of tanned leather. Phrygian miters, bronze helmets or high fur bonnets rose above foreheads. They carried yew-wood bows with slack strings, javelins, clubs or double-headed axes knotted to the wrist by a loose thong, and, as a defensive weapon, a buckler, disk- or crescent-shaped, of stretched wild ass-skin laminated with bronze.

Those whom age or wounds had rendered inapt for the service of war directed the carts of the convoy. With them marched girls who were not yet nubile, whose flock spread out alongside the roads, through the countryside, in the joy of exercise, at games of skill or strength. Some were drawing bows, menacing the flight of birds; others were wrestling one another, stripped of their tunics and bracing their slender muscles. The boldest took hold of the withers of wild stallions, bounding on to their backs, exciting them with their voices to furious gallops while hammering them with their knees. They leapt nimbly to the ground without letting go of the mane, and remounted the animals with a supple leap, enjoying their bucking. And there was laughter, combined with challenges and appeals, which rose from the dust raised by the tangle of gallops, and mingled with the whinnying of the beasts.

Meanwhile, the city appeared, profiling the whiteness of its cubic houses with terraces against the tender verdure of the meadows. The tribes formed up again. At the edge of the city, Hippolyta assigned each caravan a camp-site near a clump of trees that shaded a spring or on the banks of the Thermodon, the river with the lively waters, the sinuosities of which, after having irrigated the plain, girdled Themiscrya with a wide ditch.

At the attributed emplacement the old women unloaded the carts, milked the cows and set up the tents on the poles. The adults tethered the horses, keeping the stallions upwind of the fillies, while the aurochs gazed freely. In noisy bands, the children jostled one another while gleaning dead wood and went to fill leather bottles from springs or the river. Soon, the fires were blazing more brightly in the descending shadow, and venison procured by hunting along the route was roasting over braziers, larded with grease. Then, appetites satisfied, when night fell, everyone lay down, rolled in mats or hides and slept in the shelter of the tents, in the dying light of the fires and the vague smile of the moon.

The matinal fanfares of buccinas brought the Amazons out of their tents at dawn. Their courses brightened with green wakes the meadows lightly dusted with frost, all the way to the flowery banks of the Thermodon, which was rippled by the breeze; there they removed their tunics in order to purify themselves in the water of the river.

Bold young women ventured to traverse the river and come ashore on the other bank, or abandoned themselves to the lazy current, which bathed their bodies, as milky as the flowers of water-lilies. Crouching on the sand, the mothers washed the dainty bodies of the little girls whom the rites were about to consecrate as Amazons. The elders, near the banks, strove to retain the adolescents, and their anxious and grumbling cries scolded the recklessly mischievous individuals who evaded their surveillance in order to join their elders in the middle of the river.

Downstream, somewhat apart, members of a silent group were also bathing their newborns. That was the bleak assembly of mothers whose disinherited loins had given birth to males, and whose ailing sons were destined for the holocaust. Without regret and without tenderness, they washed the frail bodies, avoiding plunging into the water soiled by their contact and turning their dry eyes away from the reproved sexual parts. They bent themselves grimly to the humiliating task, and when it was concluded they abandoned their children on the moss in order to rejoin their companions, diving into the river upstream, impatient to purify themselves of the virile touch.

On emerging from the bath all of them dried their limbs, constellated by droplets of water and rippled by the frissons of the morning breeze, in the warmth of the rising sun. With their rounded arms they twisted the heavy waves of their wet hair, massing it on their heads like helmets.

Already, the most alert had regained the shelter of the tents, and the trampled grass of the river bank was soon deserted. Everyone was getting ready for the ritual feast. Limbs were rubbed with aromatic herbs and fards, tresses were anointed with odorous oils and the Amazons donned their tunics and belts, admiring themselves in the polish of their carefully furbished weapons as if in a mirror.

Then the crowd set forth, riotously, through the avenues, swelled at every crossroads by a new influx, spreading out over the square of the holocausts, accumulating in narrow streets and populating the plain with its life.

Hippolyta, the priestess of the Sun, stood upright in her crimson simarre, like a bloody phantom, before the monstrous pyre heaped up in the center of the circular area. In response to her order, the young mothers arranged themselves, their infants in their arms, those who had given birth to daughters to the right and those who had given birth to males to the left. The ranks of the infecund warriors ringed the sacred arena and contained the turbulent crowd of the impubescent and the curious rabble of the elders.

Penthesilea appeared on the threshold of her palace. A great acclamation went up, and the queen, pale and motionless, contemplated her people proudly. Her young beauty elevated a divine head over a harmonious body. Mars had loved her mother and the warrior nation was pleased to see its queen as a goddess, the daughter of the god of war.

She took inventory of her people with a dominating gaze, her eyes flamboyant with pride; her mouth, with lips as vivid as a wound, blossomed in a superb smile; her soul was still stained by the blood of Atys, but her smile was already defying death; her arms, outstretched horizontally, imposed on all the faces extended toward her; then they rose up vertically, as if they were bearing the soul of the nation toward the gods.

It was impossible to tell whether they were dispensing a benediction or brandishing an anathema.

But they were lowering already. At that signal the trumpets sounded and the cymbals clashed. Slowly, with a solemn stride, Penthesilea advanced, escorted by her twelve companions of honor. The respectful wave of her subjects parted before her, in order to come together again in her wake. Everyone wanted to delight in the sight of her, to touch her mantle, to respire the air that caressed her beauty. Sometimes, the queen paused, in the triumphal glory that rose up around her. Finally, she reached the steps of the altar, at the foot of which Hippolyta was waiting.

The impact of their gazes was exchanged impassively. The queen stared at the priestess for some time, and then she turned to face the Orient and prostrated herself before the god of Light. A religious wind curbed the crowd in a great silence.

Hippolyta lit the torch of the sacred fire.

With a gesture that magnified her, Penthesilea threw back the royal mantle that draped her shoulders; her bare arm, circled at the wrist and the elbow by a double gold ring, reached out and took the torch from Hippolyta's hand. Her eyes inspired, her nostrils flaring and her breast swelling, she swung the torch over the pyre, while pronouncing the sacred words. She raised it again toward the sun, as if to borrow the flames, and threw it into the mass of resinous faggots. The smoke crawled, thickened, and then rose up vertically into the placid air; the twigs crackled, and finally, bright, high flames sprang forth, and clamors of delight were rolled by the echoes.

The mothers of the male children surrounded the brazier, their naked sons in their arms. Penthesilea touched with a golden rod those reserved for a life of slavery. The priestesses emasculated them with a metallic noose and cauterized the wound.

The excised flesh was thrown into the flames as the first fruits of the holocaust. Then the newborns that Penthesilea had not marked were suspended above the fire. The queen's left hand, addressed to the heavens, descended, and that terrible gesture precipitated the victims into the hecatomb.

A shrill scream multiplied two hundred death-throes, then long wails trailed away, and there was a sudden silence . . .

Without a tear or a quiver of the entrails, the mothers moved away, to make room for their sisters, whose blessed wombs had given birth to Amazons. The girls were presented bare-breasted. The priestesses of the Sun plunged the consecrating seals into the fire, and when the seals were red-hot, with their eyes fixed on the smoke that was bearing the human incense to the heavens, they chanted the incantation of their rite:

"Sun, our Father, who laughs at our birth and puts glory on the foreheads of our daughters slain in battle, upon whom their dying eyes still fix, Sun, our Father, salutations!

"As your divine radiance warms hearts, iron burns our breast with the seal that marks us with your sign and makes us yours, O Sun our Father!

"The kiss of the Fire is your divine kiss; it puts your ardor into breasts, it magnifies in hearts the love of battles, and it gives scorn for wounds and death.

"Fire, son of the Sun our Father, O you our immortal husband, by means of the greases that aliment you, encrust in the soul and in the flesh of your daughters the glorious scorn of males; perpetuate in them the virtues of our race, forbid them the cowardice that other peoples name amour,

"Sun, our Father, and Fire, son of the Sun our Father, we adore you, light and strength, Fire, son of the Sun, and Sun, our Father."

Outside the flames the incandescent irons were fulgurant. The queen brandished the seal and applied it to the right nipple of the first child. The priestesses went to the others, who were presented by their mothers, and the juvenile flesh sizzled under the imprint of the fire.

The elders had approached; the young women handed their daughters to them, Amazons henceforth, and in exchange they received their weapons; the mothers became warriors again.

The pyre collapsed into embers; the priestesses scattered the debris of firebrands, ashes and partly-calcined bones. The rank that contained the crowd broke up and the popular rush finished sweeping the place of the holocaust under frantic trampling feet, testifying hateful disdain for the impure victims, and cries of celebration stifled in space the distant echo of plaints of agony.

Now, groups were formed for games, and hands were joined for dances. Then tables were set up, laden with meat, and Penthesilea, in the libation that she offered to the Sun, declared to Priam's envoy that she would respond to his appeal, and she ordered the departure for the following day.

The chiefs assembled their respective troops, passed the horses, harness and arms in review and gave their orders. Each detachment went to camp outside the city and made preparations for the departure.

III
On Campaign

IN the shadows, still confused, the rumor grew, populating the night. The earth awoke under trampling feet, and the whinnying of horses was heard, like bellicose appeals. Silhouettes moved, drowned in mist, accumulating at crossroads in denser masses, becoming entangled again. In response to the imperative voices of the chiefs, the swarming multitude became organized; groups formed, and the file of warrior women was soon extended along the road.

The nascent sun gradually dispelled the mist. On the summits of the hills that closed the horizon of Themiscrya, the victorious radiance unveiled the already-distant city, its whiteness vanishing in the inundation of light. With a last glance the Amazons caressed their city, and then poured down the opposite slope of the mountain, and the army's march became more emphatic, in the direction of the banks of the Scamander.

The taciturn Penthesilia went forth at the long stride of her white stallion, the reins loose around the neck. The noble beast, indocile to any other, yielded meekly to the hand of its mistress. It originated from the couple of horses born from the foam of the sea, more rapid in its course than the Harpies in their flight, a present from Orithyia, the wife of Boreas, given in gratitude for the generous hospitality once found by her in Themiscrya. The spirited horse seemed to understand and respect the Amazon's bitter reverie. However, the proud gaze of Penthesilea hid from everyone the tenebrous storms of her heart.

The day before, in the midst of the celebrations, at the head of her army and her people, the excitement of her power had heated up her Amazon blood. Her despair at the death of Atys has been attenuated, stifled by the revivified seed of her sovereignty. She hated the laws of her people, but she was proud of dominating them; she still mourned her lover, but she would no longer have gone with him. No, she would no longer have gone with him, for her departure would have placed the crown on the head of Hippolyta, and all of her resentment was concentrated on that sister whom she hated, for her superior energy and for the danger with which her ambition threatened her. Furthermore, Hippolyta was strengthened by the discovered secret; the amorous weakness of Penthesilea was a weapon for her, and who could tell whether she might not suspend it incessantly over the will of the queen, and even whether she might strike her with it one day?

That hatred, those dreads and the desire for vengeance collided in Penthesilea's soul with the mourning of her passion; the latter was magnified in order to swell the tempest and to be absorbed entirely by it. But the woman imposed upon her wrath, concentrating it, ready to burst forth at the opportune moment, enclosed in the felinity of her sex.

Thus, her will, extended toward an obscure goal, masked her incurable rancor, She pretended to be grateful to Hippolyta for the aid lent to her weakness and, appearing to recognize her superiority, ceded a large part of her command to her. She left to her the orders of the route, the choice and the installation of the camp, either according her free rein or ratifying the measures taken by the princess.

Hippolyta, surprised by her sister's prompt resignation, was disquieted by that sudden favor. Might not that abandonment of her royal prerogatives denounce a disgust for life, in which the queen, broken by events but reclaimed nevertheless by her throne, was only seeking to support her shaken strength on an energy that had revealed itself to be superior?

Imprudent Hippolyta! She had pronounced a word that Penthesilea could not forget: "After you, I will be queen!"—a terrible pronunciation that haunted the jealous hatred of the one and the ambitious hope of the other equally.

The forward march continued. The frontier had been crossed several days before; food supplies were becoming scarce and a great hunt was decided in order to restock the convoy. The country was rich in game; the next day they would not lift camp and the day would be employed in a general beating.

At dawn the huntresses were divided into two groups, trackers and beaters. The first, on horseback, was under the orders of Evadre; the second, on foot, would lie on wait for the hunted beasts and bar their route. Penthesilea would remain with the latter group, commanded by Derione.

The impetuous Hippolyta had already gone forward with Autandre, who was directing the dog pack. They described a great circle in order to take the game from the rear.

The unleashed bloodhounds ran, their noses and ground level, Before them, frightened hares fled and bustards took flight, disdained by the huntresses, who were in quest of larger prey.

With an abrupt gesture, Autandre stopped her mount on its hocks and her curt whistle rallied the mastiffs. With her extended arm she explained her pause to Hippolyta. Beyond the wood whose edge they were about to cross, in the depths of a grassy valley, a herd of wild aurochs was grazing. One of them, a giant, somewhat apart, was not grazing; its muzzle was in the air, breathing in the wind, ready to raise the alarm. Fortunately, the breeze was blowing toward the Amazons, but prudence was necessary in order to take the sagacious animal by surprise.

They retraced their steps and soon encountered Evadre and her companions; the dispositions for the attack were settled then.

The Amazons spread out in two lines, which were divided in a fashion to circle around the signaled game. Beyond the herd the lines came together and turned about, ready to advance in a gigantic pincer movement, the arms of which overlapped the herd while the reinforced center gave chase, only leaving the animals free to flee in the direction that would bring them into confrontation with Derione.

When everyone was in position, Autandre, who was placed to the right with Hippolyta, blew three times into her twisted horn. That was the signal; the horses were launched forward, maintained in their order by the Amazons.

At the unfamiliar clamors of the buccina the anxious beasts ceased grazing and listened, their necks extended; already alerted by the increasing gallop of the stallions, in response to the bellowed alarm of their guardian, the aurochs abruptly turned tail and ran.

The unleashed dogs rushed in their pursuit, stimulated by the sight of the beasts, filling the plain with their ferocious howls; the gallop of the horses accelerated and, shaking their manes, the stallions threw furious whinnies into the tempest of barking.

Driven into the fatal route by the overlap of the pincers formed by the aggressors, the animals emerged into the flat plain and precipitated their flight toward the line of trees in which Derione and her companions were lying in ambush. They went head down, the slender tips of their horns parallel to the ground, laboring the earth with their cloven hooves, harassed on the flanks by Hippolyta and Autandre, with Evadre on their heels, their hocks already bitten by the mastiffs. Enveloped, their stampede was grouped into a compact mass, the surge of which seemed irresistible, and the earth trembled under their charge.

Abruptly, they stopped; Derione's warriors, unmasked in a triple row, barred their route.

Their hesitation was brief; already, the arrows of those hunting them were landing on their backs; they spun to face them.

With a single bound they charged, horns lowered, in order to break through the menacing vice; two horses were eviscerated, but the others, better handled, avoided them with abrupt sidesteps and the warrior women struck them with their lances or their javelins. Then each Amazon pursued the animal she had wounded; sometimes, irritated by the attack, it returned to a new assault, which the huntress evaded in order to strike it again. Already, numerous aurochs were strewing the meadow with their stricken bodies; others dispersed in the distance, bellowing with anger and pain, shaking the barbed arrows that were tearing their flesh.

Hippolyta pursued a black bull, the redoubtable leader of the herd. Penthesilea, standing facing her sister, awaited the impact, a javelin in her right hand and a lance at the ready. Hippolyta pressed the gallop of her horse, jealous of the capture, her ax brandished in order to fall upon the aurochs; Penthesilea launched herself to meet her, as if to aid her victory.

The bull swerved, cutting the line between the queen and her sister; the latter, level with the beast, brought down her ax, while Penthesilea hurled her javelin.

The spear grazed the spine in its short parabola, but Hippolyta dropped her weapon and fell, unsaddled, her side traversed by the dart. With a mad charge the aurochs turned on the wounded warrior; with a furious thrust of the head it lifted the Amazon straight up, and carried away the inanimate body, stuck to its horns, transpierced by the two points.

A clamor of terror went up. The warrior women, with one surge, ran at the bull and surrounded it. The aurochs understood that retreat was impossible. It stopped, beat its flanks with its rough tail and pawed the ground with its hoof. Bristling with darts, fuming under the crimson of its wounds, it waited, raising Hippolyta's cadaver over its cranium like the trophy of its vengeance.

Already, from all sides, spears were entering its flanks; the bull, in its impassive majesty, closed its eyes and died on its feet, still hoisting the body of the Amazon. Its bellow of agony still seemed to be sounding its victory.

Penthesilea contemplated her victim mutely, and the Amazons attributed her frightful pallor to despair. But Hippolyta's eyelids fluttered, and her gaze understood. She lifted her hand in order to express a curse and opened her lips in order to speak . . .

Her agonizing strength betrayed her effort; a hoarse sigh tore her throat, and the Amazon fell back again, rigid, her lips closed eternally over the terrible accusation.

All night long, fires dotted the plain, illuminating the troop engaged in a double task. Some were piling up the faggots that would be the funeral bed of the Amazon; others were butchering the felled aurochs, cutting the flesh into large flat slices destined to be cured under saddles, and stuffing entire limbs into leather bottles of brine. The hides, carefully stripped, were taken to the pyre and formed Hippolyta's bed with their mass. Around the body, the skulls of the aurochs overlapped their sharp horns in sheaves, like a grille. The princess, clad in her weapons, reposed superbly, her open eyes terrible in death.

The silent army surrounded the pyre. There was no moan or murmur, for laments insult the manes of warriors fallen in combat. Soon the flames were swirling, puncturing the darkness with their conflagration; through the tongues of flame Hippolyta's body could be glimpsed, the sizzling of flesh detonating over their hissing. On Penthesilea's order, the singers intoned the battle hymn, and around the pyre dances unfurled to the rhythm of the heroic choruses.

The queen remained impenetrable, absorbed by the secret satisfaction of her revenge. Atya ought to be trembling with joy in his sepulcher on seeing himself thus avenged. As for her, her gravity created belief in her mourning, and the irony of her subjects' credence stimulated her savage pleasure. In sum, the secret of her recent weakness was buried forever; she would no longer tremble in her pride; all rivalry was dispelled and she felt herself to be truly the queen henceforth.

IV
Ilion

THE moon, young on the departure from Themiscrya, had broadened her smile and then decreased, sharpening her silvery horns. Three more nights went by under the somber tent of a crescent-less disk. The next day, at the hour when the sun floats at the zenith before inclining toward the sea, the ramparts of Ilion raised up their mass, drowned in vibrant light. An acclamation rose from the ranks of the warrior women,

The watchman on Mount Colone was dazzled by the reflection of weapons through the dusty haze; soon his attentive eyes saw the Amazon cavalry emerge from the valley of the Simois. His buccina drew out three long appeals, which resuscitated the city weighed down in the torpor of its siesta.

Troilus, selected by the king among his sons, had three black mares with fuming nostrils harnessed in haste, seized the reins, and launched his chariot over the paving stones.

He went at a gallop over the road crackling with sparks under the hammering of iron, and appeared thunderously before the young queen. Abruptly immobilized by the torsion of a robust wrist, the mares flexed their hocks and reared up, constellating their dark breasts with the snow of their foam. Troilus descended from the chariot, bowed, and pronounced the welcoming words:

"Queen, daughter of Mars, the divine Priam, sovereign of Ilion, my illustrious father, has sent me to you in order to bring you the speech of welcome and the actions of grace due to the aid that your arm brings to our weapons."

Impatient to penetrate the famous city of Ilus, Penthesilea interrupted:

"Hasten, young warrior, to conduct me to your father. I thank you for your message, but for me, actions are preferable. Climb into my chariot and guide us."

The warrior women went around the wall to the south, between Colone and the theater, in order to conceal their presence from the

Hellenes, and soon reached the Scaean gate, about which a noisy crowd was swarming.

The venerable Priam appeared, in the glory of his inestimable prosperity and the majesty of his old age. On his white-haired head a golden diadem radiated, like the sun surging from a snowy peak; his breast was enlarged by the ample fleece of a beard reminiscent of a silvery cascade. The whiteness stood out against the Ilian crimson with which the robe was dyed, and the aged king advanced at a slow pace, an ivory scepter in his hand, which rang against the paving stones.

Behind him the august sovereign members of his family were gathered, including the inconsolable Hecuba, haunted by the specter of her beloved son Hector, the fallen rampart of Ilion. The Greek woman Helen, arrogant and lascivious, confident in her beauty, was smiling into a polished silver mirror that a black slave carried before her incessantly, in order that she could intoxicate herself with the contemplation of her charms—charms celebrated by ten years of war and the manes of the heroes fallen for her defense or her conquest.

Andromache was isolated in the cold tomb of her mourning veils and hugged to her jealous bosom the son that Hector named

Scamandrius and the Trojans Astyanax; Polyxena was blushing, troubled by the amour with which her brother's killer charmed her. Further away was the noble Anchises, curbed by the years, and his pious son Aeneas, whose virile fist gripped the hand of young Ascanius, the hope of his divine race—for he descended from Dardanus, and Venus was his mother. In a confused mass were huddled Deiphobus, Helenus, Laodice, Creusa and Priam's other children spared by the combats.

Alone to one side, in the pallor of her white tunic, her forehead circled by the sacred bandlets, her eyes bewildered by mystery and her hair undone—the blonde hair that caused her to be compared to golden Cypris—the virgin Cassandra was compressing with her waxen hands her inspired mouth, which was never heeded.

From the height of the ramparts, palms and wreaths rained down; their verdure carpeted the ground over which the Amazons passed. With a gesture, Penthesilea stopped her troops and advanced alone toward the divine Priam.

Before the king, under the will of muscular thighs, the stallion flexed its knees. The young sovereign dismounted, took off her ring, handed it to Priam, and received his as a pledge of alliance.

Triumphal acclamations burst forth, amid the din of tympanons and cymbals; the breath of buccinas passed in gusts; the members of the crowd stamped their feet deliriously.

Mothers held out their children toward Penthesilea, confident in the virtue of her contact, and even the mere sight of her; warriors brandished and clinked their weapons and darted arrows toward the sky in the enthusiasm of imminent victories; old men extended their arms, imposing their hands in broad gestures of benediction toward the woman they called the liberator of the fatherland.

The universal joy, which carried the entire city away in the folly of hope, curbed the one inspired by the gods with fear, agitating her with a sacred frisson. Cassandra attempted to stifle the cry of her burning lips, but her will had to submit to celestial force, and like a flame springing from a blaze, like a crater tearing under the rush of infernal fires, her words broke out of her throat:

"Woe! Woe! Woe! Woe betide you, imprudent Princess! Woe betide you, children of Dardanus! Woe betide you, my race! Deaf ears and blind eyes, open, hear and see! Blood is swelling the waters of the Simois and the Scamander, the blood of Ilion and its allies.

Upon you, Princess, falls back that shed by you, shed by you! Return to the grassy banks of the Thermodon; flee your misfortune . . . ! Vain is my prayer, alas! You will never see your realm again . . . Envy the fate of your companions, whose pyres will blacken the plain; you are going to the worst of destinies! Believe, believe in me; the heavens inspire me. The Palladium is abandoning our walls, the anger of the goddess menaces the culpable nest of the infidel dove. Take the wife back to the husband; save the fatherland! Return Helen to Menelaus!"

Her voice died away; her imploring arms, stiffened toward the sky, fell back, charging Paris and his Greek woman with divine anathema; her hand touched Penthesilea's belly, stigmatizing the source of her woes.

The Amazon blanched with anger and religious horror, upset by the prophetic cry; she recoiled like a tiger preparing to pounce; but the old king, smiling, obstinate in his fatal incredulity, shook his head, placing his finger upon it.

The gesture calmed Penthesilea, and the indifference with which the populace scorned Cassandra's words dissipated her dread. The young queen did not think of taking vengeance for the words proffered by the virgin; her dementia made her sacred.

However, a shadow veiled the Amazon's brow; she had sensed the vengeful manes of Hippolyta floating over her. But the sky was pure, flowers enveloped her, a great people was acclaiming her, and the elite of her warriors promised her victory. She smiled proudly and took the hand that the king offered her.

The cortege penetrated into the walls, preceded by processions of young women and ephebes, who alternated their songs and interwove their dances. Buccinas sounded furiously, cymbals burst forth delightedly and tympanons rolled a martial din of chariots.

Penthesilea advanced by Priam's side, reveling in the ovation that rose up before her. The riches of the open temples, the splendor of the flag-decked houses and the steles fuming with aromatics struck her eyes with wonder and intoxicated her pride.

A new gate gaped and Penthesilea was inside Pergame. Broad porphyry steps rose up to the agora of the Acropolis. There stood the royal palace of black marble and the sanctuary in the depths of which the sacred Palladium was enthroned, the tutelary image that the heavens had deposited before the tent of Ilus when the ancestor, escorted fifty young men and fifty virgins of Phrygia has stopped on the hill of Até, conducted by the varicolored heifer.

Three cubits high, the wooden statue was raised on its united feet, severe amid the riches of the temple. Its right hand brandished a lance, its left held a spindle and distaff, the symbolic attributes of the strength of nations, the strength created by the valor of warriors and the labor of citizens.

Victims with gilded horns, decorated with bandlets and anointed with cinnamon, were awaiting the sacrificer's knife: a holocaust destined to seal the alliance and obtain the good graces of the goddess; but on the threshold, Penthesilea stopped. The terrace deployed its horizon all the way to the distant sea. The Amazon turned her impatient face toward the country and remained motionless, obstinate in the fascinating vision

Out there, toward the blue line of the waters, the shore was bristling with Argian hulls, beyond the retrenchment, the sinuosities of which were already evoking a plan of battle in the brain of the warrior woman. She inspected the area that separated her from the enemy, reconnoitering the undulations and the plains. A flame lit up in her eyes and the generous blood of her veins warmed her cheeks. Her gesture enveloped the pullulation of the Hellenic army, from the point of Sigea to the mouths of the Scamander.

The king enumerated the heroes and the peoples in coalition against holy Ilion. At Cape Rhoete were the two Ajaxes, the son of Oileus and the son of Telamon, whom the river isolated from the rest of the army. In the far distance, in the last rank, was Agamemnon, the king of kings, and next to him his brother Menelaus, the husband of that Helen whose beauty justified the war. Closer were the wily Ulysses and the temeritous Diomedes, whose lance was crimsoned with divine blood, for the warrior had wounded Cypris. There were others, and at the very extremity, covering the right wing of the besiegers at the promontory of Sigea, was the most terrible, the most handsome and the most valiant: Achilles, the vanquisher of the invincible Hector.

And the voice that had quivered in pronouncing the name of the hero, the son of the goddess of the sea, now named the races: the Athenians, the most civilized of the Greeks; the Phoceans, bold explorers of the seas; the superb Argians; the Locrians who fought with spears; the Dulichians, skillful with the sling; the Dolopes; the Epeans; the Beotians and the Myrmidons commanded by Achilles; those who came from the continent and the islands, and the other peoples composing the hundred thousand warriors whom, ten years before, eleven hundred and eighty-six ships had poured out under the ramparts of Ilion.

The old king and the young Penthesilea were lost in their contemplation, forgetful of the holocaust. Priam was agonizing over past terrors, the mournings that were bleeding within him, but then he stiffened himself for the vengeance; the Amazon was bounding toward the offered glory, excited by her imminent triumph over such heroes, whom men had been unable to vanquish.

And her voice clamored her challenge:

"Proud Argians, the daughter of Mars has come to vanquish you. You will be swept away by her hurricane, precipitated into the waters that your reckless hulls have labored. Not one of you will see again the lands were your widows and your mothers are weeping sterile tears. Superb Agamemnon, I shall deprive you of your scepter; astute Ulysses, I shall break your ruses; imprudent Diomedes, I shall avenge the blood of the gods. And you, son of Thetis, who call yourself indomitable, I shall teach you to know what the arm of a woman weighs. Venerable Priam, my illustrious host, open your heart wide to joy; your woes will be avenged and the city will grow over the ossuary of your enemies. The god, my father, inspires me, and his strength is in me!"

Her breast rose as her fists brandished an anathema; her eyes were flamboyant, like lightning amid clouds projecting the thunderbolts held in its claws by the eagle of the god of gods. The crowd fell silent religiously; only Cassandra trailed her tearful lament over the parvis of the temple.

Penthesilea took the king's right arm again and penetrated into the sanctuary. Voices burst forth under the porticos intoning the hymn of the goddess, and the triumphal chant swept away the prophetic plaint.

Theano, the wife of Antenor, the priestess of Athena with the cerulean eyes, lifted the bronze cutlass and cut the throats of the victims. One by one they fell, immolated by a sure stroke, piling up before the table of holocausts; the blood was collected by Theano's acolytes in bowls of gold, agate and onyx.

Priam guided Penthesilea to the altar; their extended hands were united above the fuming pool; they plunged together into the accumulated blood; the queen's finger imprinted her sigil on Priam's forehead; he marked the Amazon's uncovered breast at the same time. They were then indissolubly united in the thought that is concerted, in the heart that decides, and the hand that acts.

The palace of Paris, adjacent to the king's, had been adapted for Penthesilea and her companions. Helen had not been able to refuse that homage to the warrior women who were sustaining her quarrel.

Priam invited his allies to a sumptuous feast. The immense room, sustained by a hundred columns ten cubits high, accommodated the Amazon army, the fifty sons of Priam, his twelve daughters, their husbands and the illustrious chiefs of Ilion.

Penthesilea, ardent for combat, did not linger over pleasure. She wanted to enter into campaign at dawn. As soon as the shades of night spread over the city she stood up and ordered the army to repose.

V
The Battle

THE pallors of dawn were opalizing the indecisive line of the horizon when a dark cloud, trailing like a mist, awoke a tempestuous rumor that grew into a deafening din, like the multiple clash of blades hammered like the beating of iron on innumerable anvils. Already a furious cavalcade was emerging from the tearing curtain of dust.

On the backs of their horses, which they excited with their voices and stimulated with their heels, the warrior women charged, clad in crimson tunics, dyed with that bloody color in order to dissimulate their wounds, their unbound hair rippling in the wind of their course and darts glinting in their brandished fists. Their flying line extended its wings immeasurably, enclosing within its gigantic span the salient of the retrenchment that covered the troops of Antilochus.

The ditch, eight cubits deep and sixteen wide, was coupled with an embankment whose narrow rim was bristling with a network of pointed stakes fixed by solid ropes. The crest was crenellated, reinforced by high wooden towers that flanked the dead corners. The surge of the Amazons had to break against that insurmountable obstacle.

In the rear, the slender masts projected of ships beached on the strand, wedged on their stanchions and swelling their rostra. Before their triple line the huts of the Hellenes were grouped, the mud walls of which sustained oblique roofs of rushes and fascines. The besiegers were sleeping in complete quietude, and the charge arrived just as the guards posted in the towers gave the first alarm.

At the level of the trench in which the charge seemed sure to be engulfed, the stallions stopped and reared up, enlarging their foamy breasts and beating the air with their unshod hooves. A volley of javelins, in a skillful parabola, skimmed the top of the parapet and plowed a murderous furrow through the disorderly host of warriors who were rushing to the ramparts.

Already, with a prompt about-turn, the stallions were carrying away their audacious mistresses, whose retreat vanished in the turbulence of their dusty wake, in which the impotent flight of the arrows launched by the enemies of Ilion died.

While the latter, alarmed by the abruptness of the attack, equipped themselves in haste, and took away the dead and wounded who had fallen under the cloud of Amazon darts, the warrior women reformed and renewed their maneuver at another section of the wall. Having launched their javelins they retreated again, pursued by the malediction that their enemies hurled at them in the sterile explosion of their wrath.

Mounted on her white stallion, whose course equaled a flight, Penthesilea multiplied herself among her troops, rallying them in the retreat and bringing them back to the attack. After the first skirmishes she divided them into six echelons, commanded, under her, by Clonie, Polemusa, Derione, Evadre, Autandre and the divine Bremusa; she kept with her Thermodusa of the invincible lance and the beautiful Harmothoa. Behind the queen were grouped Alcibia, Antrobota, Hippothoa and Derimarque, ready to transmit her orders and to cover her with their bodies.

Penthesilea lifted up her curved buckler, which rose into the air like Phoebe's crescent. At that signal, Clonie led her troop forward.

Having recovered from the stupor of the first attack, the Hellenes had crossed the ditch and deployed in the plain. The Amazon charge broke through their ranks, still devoid of cohesion, but before they had reached the bridges of the enclosure, the enemy reinforcements flowed out and drowned them in the melee.

At a sign from the queen, Bremusa and Derione launched forward to aid Clonie; their impetuous impact disengaged their companions. The Greeks were felled in their course like ears of corn under the harvester's scythe; they lay on the ground numerously, among them Anathée, Lerne, Hypalme, Emonide and Elasippe,[1] celebrated for their prowess. Laogon stopped the surge of Derione's horse with a firm hand, hanging on to the bridle; with a stroke of her ax, the furious Amazon severed the head of the reckless warrior, whose free hand was clutching her leg, attempting to

---

1 This list of names, which I have given as the *Nouvelle Revue* text does, and a few other elements of this chapter, are taken from a *suite* [sequel or continuation] to the *Iliad* appended to the French translation of the epic by François Du Souhait (c1575-1617), a prolific author of pastiche romances.

unsaddle her. Laogon remained standing for a moment, then vacillated and collapsed like a felled oak.

Clonie attacks Menippe, the proud companion of Protesilas; the Hellene evades the impact and thrust with his spear, which arrests the Amazon's pelta. She spins around, profits from the shock that had exposed Menippe in his thwarted effort, and plants a sure thrust in his heart. The warrior's hands clench in order to extract the iron, and then part, beating the air, and his life is exhaled through the unbridled wound.

Clonie utters a cry of triumph, to which the vengeful clamor responds of the son of Iphicles, Podarchus, the friend of the fallen warrior; who will replace his dear companion in his tent? With one bound he implants himself on the rump of the horse; his muscular arms girdle the Amazon, his rebounding feet stimulate the gallop of the stallion toward the camp, to which he carries his prey away.

Bremusa has launched herself in pursuit of the abductor; entirely absorbed by her chase, she does not see Idomeneus, whose lance reopens the scar of her infecund nipple; her life flows away in the bloody spring and the daughter of the gods dies on her horse, which carries the cadaver off toward Ilion, the knees clutching its flanks.

Without ceasing to strike with great blows, Penthesilea has sent Evadre and Thermodusa to replace their sisters at the head of their troops. Scarcely have they entered the melee than Merionus launches a javelin between the leg of Evadre's horse; the beast falls and the warrior woman rolls on the sand, stunned. Merionus has her carried away from the battle, tied up, but Thermodusa rushes him; he evades her attack, breaking her lance with a reverse sweep of his sword. Disarmed, she tries to flee; Merionus cuts the hamstrings of her mare, which falls, and delivers Thermodusa to the victor.

Carried away by their impetuosity, separated from their companions, Alicibia and Derione, enveloped by the enemy ranks, as tightly packed as the waves of the sea, wreak great carnage around them; blood pours from their multiple wounds; they continue striking, but the numbers overwhelm them; their strength fails and, tipped from their mounts, they go to share the captivity of their sisters.

Meanwhile, the Trojans have emerged from the walls and advanced to aid their allies. Penthesilea, irritated by the loss of her warriors, runs to meet them, places herself at their head, excites them with her inflamed speech and draws them in her wake. Glaucus places himself next to her, his heart given to the daughter of Mars, seduced by her beauty; he wants to fight before her eyes, to conquer her by force of glory, and to protect her life. Derimarque charges with them. Antribota, Hippothoa, Polemusa and Autandre, under the orders of Harmothoa, remain in reserve with the last Amazons to watch over the security of the flanks and aid any threatened positions.

The collision of the two armies rumbled in the plain like thunder in the melee of the clouds. Before Penthesilea the enemy line scattered like a flock of starlings on which a vulture swoops.

Suddenly, Ajax and his warriors emerge on the right flank of the assailants. Boldly, Harmothoa launches forward, followed by Polemusa, Autandre and their squadrons. Irresistibly, their impetus introduces them like a wedge into the broken ranks; they strew a frightful massacre in their wake. But the son of Telamon orders his men to open a broad passage; the warriors part before the charge in order to reclose their ranks behind the imprudent Amazons; they soon find themselves alone, for their troops have not been able to follow their frenzied charge. The stallions succumb, struck from behind, and an ironic clamor salutes the fall and capture of the Amazons.

A dolorous cry erupts from Hippothoa's breast: "Sister," she shouts to Antribota, "vengeance is ours!"

Immediately, they fall upon Ajax, the reins in their teeth, club and spear in hand; but fortune belies their valor; the hero has awaited them, calm behind his buckler; his long lance rips out Hippothoa's entrails; but Antrobota attains him; irritated by the stroke, which has marked his forehead with a bloody furrow, he turns and strikes the temeritous arm that has struck him with a sweep of his sword, and then, falling upon the stricken warrior woman, he plunges his blade into her breast.

Achilles joins Ajax, carving a bloody swathe through the battle. At an impetuous gallop, Penthesilea's stallion brings the queen to encounter the heroes, and her presence re-establishes the combat. Alone, she confronts Achilles and Ajax. The latter, brushed by an arrow, disdains the Amazon; Achilles will suffice for the victory. But Glaucus has hurled himself upon him; the son of Telamon deflects his spear and pierces his breast; the valiant

Trojan, dying, darts one last amorous glance at Penthesilea as his eyes are invaded by eternal darkness.

Derimarque, the last companion of the young queen, wards off the mortal blow with which Achilles threatens Penthesilea, white with horror. Furious, like a wild boar deflected from its prey, the son of Thetis fells with a javelin the audacious woman who has raised an obstacle to his victory.

Penthesilea, hot with vengeance, brandishes her fist and menaces the hero's heart with a dart. Achilles raises the buckler from Etna and the dart breaks on the metal forged by a god.

"The second will be surer!" vociferates the queen. "Dare you, mortal, measure yourself against the daughter of Mars? You shall tell the shades what an Amazon is."

Lance at the ready, Achilles awaits the impact of Penthesilea. The point, turned away by the pelta, nevertheless tears her shoulder. Wounded, the Amazon drops the heavy ax suspended over her enemy's skull.

The queen, mad with rage, unsheathes her sword; the weapon breaks on the hero's helmet. Under the formidable shock the latter totters, falls to one knee, and a tempest of triumph and fear passes over the two armies.

Penthesilea rushes to complete her victory. The crouching warrior braces himself on his lance.

With an adroit thrust he strikes the horse in the breast. The iron emerges from the withers and penetrates the warrior woman's side. The expiring stallion beats the air with its hooves and falls backwards, crushing the Amazon's body with its weight.

A desperate plaint springs from the decimated ranks of the warrior women. They rush to save their queen, or at least to protect her remains from profanation; but, deprived of her, they fall one by one, without retreating, under the blows of the enemy.

Panic had carried Priam's army all the way to the walls, shaking the air with cries of terror; it seemed to all of them that they had seen Hector die for a second time.

Achilles, his foot on Penthesilea's breast, insulted her impotence.

"Daughter of a god, you have succumbed to the son of a goddess. Why did you not remain with the women? You know now what a hero is; your weapons will enrich the tent of Achilles."

He leans over, detaches the thongs that fasten Penthesilea's golden helmet. He retains his weapon, dazzled by her beauty. Grimly, she darts her gaze at him, but a radiance effaces their flash of hatred; a divine vision makes Atys live again in her conqueror.

She closes her eyelids and seals her lips on the imprecation that rises from her heart. Already, she accepts her slavery.

VI
The Hut of Achilles

IN the hut of heavy trunks of fir-wood, covered with reeds, in a large hall sustained by forks and divided by curtains, Achilles was absorbed in the contemplation of his captive, lying almost lifeless on heaped-up fleeces. The beauty of the warrior woman filled his eyes and penetrated his heart. He was moved by an immense regret for his strength, and he cursed the hand that had dealt the blow, perhaps mortal, to the woman who had made him cherish life.

Alone among all women, she seemed to him to be worthy of sharing his bed, of bearing his lineage in her womb, as much by virtue of her beauty as her valor. The charming body of a woman was insufficient for a man such as him; to fill the heart of the hero it required the soul of a heroine.

Impatiently, he stood up, lifted the curtain of the entrance and gazed into space. He adjured the gods, irritated by the slowness of Automedon, whom he had dispatched to Machaon, the divine son of Aesculapius, the most skillful man in the army in the army in the knowledge of the plant juices that can heal wounds.

He finally appeared; Achilles ran to him and brought him to the couch on which Penthesilea lay.

Machaon washed the wound and sounded its depth. He anointed her lips with a marvelous balm, covered it with a liniment of crushed herbs collected at midnight by moonlight, and sacred words quivered in his mouth without it yielding their secret.

Somberly, Briseis crouched at the back of the tent, enveloping her master and his prisoner with a jealous gaze. Already she had suffered in her heart on seeing Achilles' amour go toward Polyxena, who had troubled the hero during Hector's funeral.

Is this the Achilles, she asked herself, bitterly, *who stood up to Agamemnon and broke with the army in order to have me for himself?*

That memory reanimated her hope slightly; she crawled slowly, slid her young arms around the warrior's knees, and raised her imploring face toward him, its tears divinized by amour. Achilles, entirely absorbed by his dolor, pushed her away with a harsh hand.

"Master," she sighed, "why do you scorn my tenderness?"

"Because you're only a slave."

"And what is this one?" growled Briseis, in a voice of revolt.

"This one is a queen."

"I was a princess."

"You're only a woman. She alone thought she could vanquish me."

"She is your enemy."

"No," roared Achilles, "no: my rival! Do you think, poor girl, that the wild beast couples with the ewe? The lion takes the ewe, but he loves the lioness. A female is not sufficient for the true male; he needs a companion."

"What am I then, for you?"

"You are the one who washes the feet, prepares the meals, smoothes the garments and serves the master's pleasure. You are the slave."

"And if she dies?"

"Don't crow about that; I'll immolate you to her manes. So, remember that your life depends on hers. Have no illusions about the power of your charms; I swear that holocaust by the Styx, the oath of the gods, the oath of Achilles."

Briseis got up grimly; soon she slipped outside the hut through the door that stood ajar, leaving Achilles at Penthesilea's bedside.

The sand-glass had been trickling its grains into the inferior globe for a long time when a rumor, distant at first, came closer, like a breaking wave. Cries troubled the hero in his anxious contemplation; he listened, and recognized the shrill voice of the impostor Thersites inciting the tumult.

The racket swelled and amassed before his shelter. Among the vociferations rang his name and that of Penthesilea. The wretch was rousing the soldiers against the hero, the protector of the Amazon, the cruel enemy who had afflicted the army with so much mourning that very day. Thersites enumerated the valiant men slain, exciting the crowd to demand the captive and sacrifice her on the pyre of the dead, to satisfy their manes and enable their shades to rejoice.

The heavy door, which only shifted slowly to the effort of three men, flew open at the push of the hero. Achilles appeared, without weapons. The mob recoiled before his angry face. Careless of the threats, he marched straight to Thersites, raised his fist and brought it down. The skull of the mischief-maker shattered, splashing the ground with his brains.

The hero mastered the rabble with his gaze, and returned disdainfully to his hut.

Briseis had taken advantage of Achilles' brief exit to slip into the hut. She was waiting, spying on the result of her scheming. Ashamed, she saw Thersites fall. In vain she had lowered herself to promising her favors to the vilest of the Hellenes. She took refuge on her mat, fearful of her master's vengeance, but the warrior had not even noticed her absence.

Reassured, Briseis exhausted the night in inane sighs; the heart of the hero did not deign to hear them. Dawn found Achilles still watching over Penthesilea's slumber.

Machaon returned to examine the wound, bandaged it, and withdrew silently.

However, a sigh palpitated on the lips of the captive. Her eyelids fluttered, unveiling pupils in which the vision of Achilles burned. Neither the victor nor the vanquished spoke, but their exchanged gazes radiated in their hearts.

In the depths of his palace, the old king of Ilion was plunged in his despair of victory. His faith, shaken by the death of Hector, foundered forever in the defeat of Penthesilea. Strength ebbed away from him, and he renounced it in order to struggle by means of cunning. The alliance of his daughter Polyxena, whom he knew that Achilles loved, would deprive the besiegers of the hero who protected their arms. His defection would lead to the retreat of the Hellenes or ensure their ruination. The gods had predicted it. Pergame would not fall without Achilles.

Priam shuddered at the thought of uniting the sister to her brother's bloody murderer; but the salvation of the fatherland would affirm his tottering throne; reasons of State conquered him in the end, imposing their rights upon him, and his decision was made.

A secret messenger took the king's words to the son of Peleus. Priam invited the chief to the honor of his hospitality. Achilles accepted, out of pride.

However, the evoked image of Polyxena passed before his eyes, discolored, as distant as that of the slave banished from his bed. The Amazon reigned alone within him.

Achilles ordered Briseis to furbish the weapons forged by Vulcan: the buckler with five creases, marvelously sculpted, encrusted with bronze, silver and gold, the edges of which resembled the urgent waves of the sea; the breastplate more flamboyant than the brazier of a forge; the helmet with a golden crest dazzling with gems; the jugulars of superimposed metallic plates covered with emeralds; the sword with the inflexible blade; the ten-cubit lance with the point inlaid with gold. And to humiliate the restive slave further, when she presented the weapons to him, he cut off her long hair to make a mane for his crest.

His chariot and his caparisoned horses were waiting for him. Suddenly, he pushed the reins away and went back into his hut. He could not determine himself to depart while Penthesilea's life was in danger. In his irresolution, amour prevailed. He sent a herald to Priam to adjourn acceptance of his offer under the pretext of illness. Strong in that pretence, he enclosed himself and devoted all his hours to the wounded woman.

Life, momentarily suspended, took hold of the Amazon again. With the renascent strength, her reaffirmed pride struggled against the servitude of her heart. Exhausted by the malady, she had abandoned herself to the charm of sensing, trembling beside her, the hero who made the earth tremble. The supernatural beauty of the man had evoked in her the memory of and desire for amorous joys. Now that dolor was no longer repressing her thought, the confession of her amour revolted the vanquished woman; she would have liked to struggle, to have her revenge, to be victorious over her conqueror. A cruel triumph! A perilous combat, the blows of which would come back against the woman who had dealt them! And yet she, the sovereign, was no more than a slave! Oh yes, she was a slave, more subjugated by her heart than by her captivity.

She was indignant at her cowardice, and hid beneath the night of her eyelids the shame of her desire. A sudden oppression widened her eyes in order to stare at the danger. Achilles was leaning over her.

His tall stature was curbed, his terrible eyes had the mildness of dawn, his mouth descended upon the mouth of the Amazon. With a supreme effort, she tried to retract her lips, but in the breath of the hero they opened.

And in that kiss he drank her soul.

"You shall be queen!"

She admired him.

"You will be the companion of Achilles; you alone are made to conceive his sons."

"Oh, my lord," she sighed, raising her caressant hands to his glorious face.

"I have ransomed the captives, your companions. They will live near to you, reminding you of your homeland. Your warriors are not a race of slaves. They will live free and will form our guard. As soon as your wound is healed, my ships will inflate their sails and we shall depart for my kingdom. You have lost your throne, but you shall have that of Achilles. I'm weary of the war. Let Menelaus avenge his insult and reconquer his Helen! I have you, and I only want to live henceforth for your amour."

"King, if your hand has wounded me, your words are curing my wound, your amour is recreating my life."

In the frankness of his great heart, the warrior confessed his ephemeral inclination for Polyxena and the promise he had made to accept the hospitality of Priam.

Penthesilea was alarmed.

"I will go," the hero declared. "Achilles does not break his word. But have no fear, you alone will be the queen of my kingdom."

"Beware of a trap," insinuated the Amazon. "Those rogues the Trojans are attracting you to their home in order to rid themselves of the only enemy who makes them tremble, in order to avenge the death of their Hector."

"They would not dare! And I have my weapons."

"Against an entire people?"

"Achilles does not fear an army."

"I tremble for you, for me . . ."

"I have faith in Priam; the old man fears the gods. I will go tomorrow. The presence of your warriors will fill your wait. We will make ready to sail when I return."

The majesty of the hero stopped Penthesilea's pleas. The proud Amazon reproached herself for her anxiety, without expelling it from her heart.

Only accompanied by Automedon, Achilles departed in his chariot. Grave and silent, bearing their servitude heavily, but with proud eyes, Clonie, Evadre, Thermodusa, the beautiful Harmothoa, Polemusa and Autandre came to join their queen. Alcibia and Derione had died of their wounds.

Mutely, they arranged themselves and waited, motionless, for Penthesilea to speak.

Before the severity of her subjects, the queen dared not make the confession of her amour. In spite of her elevation on a throne, they would not pardon their princess for giving herself a master. Penthesilea only announced to them that they would not be consecrated to the baseness of servitude. They would form a royal guard under her command; they would have their weapons and would remain warriors.

A superb glint lit up in their eyes, but their foreheads remained clouded by a shadow. They were thinking about the loss of their homeland, of their liberty, of their posterity, impossible henceforth, for they would never open their arms to men in a land of which they were not the masters.

Penthesilea penetrated their thought, and blood burned her face.

She also understood that they all envied their sisters killed in battle, Defeat was worse for them than death, in their noble love of the free life.

That pride denounced to Penthesilea the decadence of her soul. She shuddered that the idea of the reprobation with which those of her race would scourge her; in their midst, the bloody shade of Hippolyta rose up, vengefully, to pursue and curse her . . .

Horrible fear chilled her limbs; desperately, she evoked her amour and warmed herself in its sunlight.

VII
The Death of the Hero

AT the gallop of his mares, Achiles furrowed the plain that he had swept with the cadaver of Hector, and the memory of the hero immolated to his anger did not alter his serenity. He crossed the ford of the Scamander and hailed the guards at the Scaean Gate. The Trojans swung its heavy bars and hauled on its chains; slowly, the massive battens yielded, opening the way. The chariot rolled under the vaults like thunder, rattling on the paving stones, and only stopped before the enclosure of Pergame.

There, Aeneas was waiting for the announced guest. Achilles abandoned his horses to Automedon and went through the postern of the Acropolis.

The son of Anchises guided the hero up the marble steps all the way to the agora, and introduced him into the steam-rooms that warmed the perfumed water of the baths. Naked slaves, daughters of the incomparable race of Taurus, undressed the hero, bathed him in the pool and, when the ablutions were terminated, massaged his muscular limbs with their expert hands. They rubbed his skin with electrum polishers and anointed the curls of his beard and hair with aromatic oils. Then they conducted him to a bed of repose and stood before him, awaiting his desire, but their beauties left the hero insensible; he did not deign to see them.

They drew away silently for the lapse of a sand-glass flow, then returned to present him with a white tunic in a fabric worthy of Arachne, embroidered with magical flowers, a silk robe twice dipped in the brightest crimson, sandals of fine esparto, and a lotus wreath to adorn his head.

Achilles rejected the effeminate garments and blushed at the memory of his exile in Scyros. He put on his armor, which did not weigh upon his strength at all.

An escort of young men came to fetch him, and introduced him into the palace. Achilles appeared before Priam; the old man rose to his feet to embrace his guest and then sat him down on the throne to his right.

Standing on the steps was Polyxena, florid with modesty, her bosom semi-veiled by the pearls of necklaces, her shoulders caressed by the long golden trellises of pendant earrings and her slender arms weighed down by amber bracelets overlaid with silver rings and cornelian beads; her fingers were burdened by shiny rings. An ivory plaque encrusted with sardonyxes fastened a girdle beneath her breasts, the roundness of which expanded their juvenile firmness. Her eyelashes, elongated by gum and antimony, shadowed her timid eyes; vermilion enlivened the tender and discreet smile of lips whose light breath exhaled amour.

Achilles smiled. The virginal smile of the young princess vanished in the radiant splendor of the queen that he had chosen.

The doors opened and the assembly penetrated into the banqueting hall.

Extended on the royal bed, the warrior, habituated to the rude frugality of the camps and the simplicity of his hut, relaxed in the luxury of the wines, dishes, flowers, candles and aromatics. He stood up and filled a cup with golden wine for a libation to the gods.

In honor of his guest, Priam seized in his turn a vase with handles decorated with the head of the symbolic owl and offered the liquor to Athena; then the two chiefs exchanged their cups and emptied them.

On pottery of polished earthenware, bright red emphasized by black decorations as shiny as onyx, slaves crowned with orchids and lotuses served fat oysters, bivalve mussels, aquatic snails twisted in spirals, orbicular scallops with dentellate shells and pyramidal sea-hares, from which the guests extracted the flesh, of marine flavors, with the aid of sharpened fish-bones. Cups of horn circled with silver, sculpted ivory and varnished clay spread the odorous soul of the crimson and golden wines that scintillates in their hollows.

The tables were laden with turtles cooked in their shells, tuna drowned in sesame oil and flat rays lightly stewed in sweet wine and sprinkled with cumin.

Large vessels with handles contained sponges steeped in odorous water acidulated with lemon juice for purifying the greasy fingers of the guests.

In order to stimulate thirst, slaves presented salads of anchovies and olives, fish-eggs marinated in brine, and with the roast meats the wine flowed. Around stuffed suckling pigs and antelopes grilled over hot stones were piled hares and quarters of wild boar, fallow deer and red deer. And there were wild geese, fat bustards and marsh teals lying on beds of large beans with black rinds, chickpeas and lentils.

Finally, there were gilded pastries kneaded with maize and millet flour, coated with marshmallow; fresh juicy watermelons; baskets of red grapes, soft figs and dried pomegranates whose peel, split like laughter, showed pink seeds.

In addition to the fumes of wines and meats, the atmosphere was thickened by effluvia spread by bunches of lotus, marshwort, centaury, blue irises like bright eyes, saffron crocuses, colchicums and orchids; to those scents were added the headier ones of aromatics; on agate steles, incense, cinnamon and electrum were fuming on bronze tripods.

Achilles was bewildered by the floating intoxication; he drank, his vague eyes dazzled. The light of suspended lamps illuminated frissons in the polish of vases, the silver of cups, the metal of spatulas and sparkling fabrics. Then the pure voices of lyres resonated, with the trill of flutes and the babble of citharas; airy, voluptuous, enchanting songs rose above the rhythmic chants. The hero yielded to their magic; forgetful of martial fanfares, he was lulled by their dissolving symphonies, and suddenly, his armor felt heavy.

To the clash of cymbals the dancers entered. To a gentle rhythm they glided languidly, their bare arms raised, their palms behind the flexible napes from which their long hair fell, anointed with perfumes, all the way to their loins.

The cadence accelerated. They straightened up, their arms rounded at the hips, and fluttered like a swarm of bees over flowers. A sigh vibrated in the harps; the hands surged forth in supplication to broaden out, extended by the hymn of amour that the flutes were modulating; their eyes were drowned in ecstasy, their lips palpitated with kisses. A river of sensuality flowed from the seven strings of the lyres; then, all the instruments were unleashed, breathing an oaristys; veils quivered, floating, strewed the floor, while they appealed for amour, swooning.

Achilles had risen to his feet, his arms open, but the dancers had disappeared; alone before him, in the whiteness of her veils, was Polyxena.

In her tremulous hands she was holding the cup of betrothal, her forehead inclined as a pledge of submission; she slaked her thirst with the beverage and then held the goblet up to Achilles' lips.

He drank.

Polyxena raised the empty cup and inverted it.

Joy burst forth, triumphantly. The pact of alliance was concluded, the betrothal irrevocable.

Paris smiled proudly. His arm sustained Hecuba, whose face was shadowed by horror. She contemplated him anxiously, read his resolution in his gaze and her wide eyes blazed bloodily. But the glint died away; her faith in that blustering and pusillanimous son was dead.

At a solemn pace she marched toward the fiancés and imposed her arms between them.

"She will only be yours," she said, "with the benediction of the gods. You will receive her from my hands in the temple of Apollo at the hour when Phoebe, his divine sister, pours her fecund light from the zenith."[1]

---

1 The Titaness Phoebe, whose name was applied to the moon, is usually represented as Apollo's grandmother, his sister being Artemis (Diana in the Roman appellation).

Expansive, the bright face ascended in the ether vibrant with stars; its rays spread their melancholy over the plain and streamed along the white walls, the heights of the terraces and the domes. The ululation of owls broke the silence with their plaintive cries, to which the suppliant voices of invisible toads replied.

Achilles, alone in the night, was haloed by lunar light; his forehead, weighed down by winy fumes, was offered to the kisses of the breeze; his lungs dilated more capaciously in the light air, embalmed with nocturnal exhalations; his footsteps, slowed slightly by the feast, ringing on the paving stones, hastened toward the temple where sensuality awaited him. He reached the porch and penetrated into the sanctuary. His desire had anticipated the hour; Phoebe was inclining, without yet abandoning the ascension of her course. The warrior, out of breath, leaned back against the porphyry of a cippus.

In the peace of the night, the religious meditation of the temple and the emptiness of the wait, his thought was liberated. Vague at first, but soon becoming more precise, the evocation of the captive who was waiting for him in the camp, amorous and confident, haunted his heart. Ardently, his lips invoked her name:

"Penthesilea!"

But his voice choked; he remembered the oath pronounced in drunkenness, the cup presented by Polyxena that bound him to the young princess; he remembered, and his indomitable soul knew fear for the first time.

He rebelled against the reality; he did not know how to retreat, so he thought of over-coming the obstacle. Was his heart of a demi-god not large enough for a double amour?

But he had sworn. The oath of the gods had been the oath of Achilles; he was bound by the Styx to the Amazon alone, and Jupiter himself trembled at the temptation of perjury . . .

The doors widened, the sanctuary blazed with a flamboyance of light; white processions of virgins awoke the sonorous vaults with their chants; lyres and citharas quivered, blue-tinted volutes of aromatics blurred the dazzle with their odorant mist. Guided by Hecuba, Polyxena, ornamented with the diadem of a princess, the snowy tunic of a virgin and crimson bandlets evocative of weddings and maternities, came toward Achilles . . .

The hero was still hesitant. Now he found the bride beautiful, and desire troubled his senses, overexcited by the orgy, rebelling against the remorse that was turning his thoughts upside down. He could not resolve to reject the joy offered, to deprive himself of the promised caresses, and his bewildered conscience sought an excuse in the recent engagement of betrothal. After all, could he deny the words exchanged, insult Priam and scorn his alliance . . . ?

He remained motionless, incapable of either a consent and a refusal. The virgin was still advancing . . . and when she touched him, he drew her to his heart.

She abandoned herself, modest and amorous. Suddenly, in the serene night, lightning flashed and the rumble of thunder growled divine wrath.

Achilles broke his embrace, and pushed Polyxena away with his stiff arms.

"The will of the gods separates us!"

He pronounced those words in a profound voice, prolonged and inflated by the echoes. A stupor suspended breaths.

Hecuba was indignant.

"Have you come to bring shame into the house of your host, perfidious individual?"

"The gods have spoken."

"You bound yourself in their name."

"They reprove my marriage. Do you dare to revolt against them, Queen?"

Her arms palpitating under her veils like white wings, Cassandra, her eyes ablaze and her face livid, uttered her cry of horror.

"O folly of men! Your blindness is leading you to the tomb. Heed the order of the gods! Go, Achilles, flee toward your ships, the land of the children of Ilus are fatal to you; and your doom will drag down the illustrious lineage of Dardanus. The celestial lightning has spoken. But still my voice is vain; no one escapes his destiny."

"Shut up!" growled Hecuba.

She marched toward Achilles.

"Traitor and perjurer, murderer of my son, will you strike me again in my daughter?"

"I fear the gods."

"Fear men."

That cry sprang forth in the vibration of a broken string. Achilles tottered and fell to his knees, his heel torn by an arrow. From the shadows that drowned the depths of the temple Paris surged forth, brandishing his bow.

The wounded man roared, pulled the arrow out of his wound, and stood up on the paving stones, which were bloodied by a black flood. He drew his sword and gathered himself to pounce, but his strength fled through the open wound; he fell back; his fist released the sword, the impact of which split the marble.

"The gods will avenge me, traitor to your guest, coward of cowards!"

Paris, leaning forward, insulted the impotent agony of his victim. He sniggered:

"Is a perjurer a guest and a worthy man? The arrow that struck you is that of Apollo; the god lent me his bow in order to avenge on you my brother, my sister and my wife."

"The wife of your abduction!"

"Of my conquest!"

"Son of a sow!"

"Bastard of a goddess prostituted to men!"

With a superb effort, Achilles rose to his feet. His disarmed hand slapped Paris in the face, stigmatizing him with its bloody imprint; then, having administered justice for the insult, he fell, having died on his feet, the death of heroes.

VIII
The New Master

RENOWN, the lame messenger of joy, flies to the Greek camp to bring the irreparable mourning. Fear weighs upon all heads, crushing the souls of warriors under the excess of the burden. All despair, still incredulous; for them, Achilles could not die.

Wandering in the night, men meet up, taciturn. Around Agamemnon's fire the assembled chiefs contemplate one another, and not one feels in his chilled marrowbones the strength to break the lamentable silence. The breath of death seems to have horrified eyes and sealed lips.

A hoarse breath, however, rumbled in the breast of Ajax; abruptly, he leapt up, his sword drawn.

"Battle!"

Fists clenched on hilts. With a gesture, Ulysses restrained the wrath.

"The oracles have spoken. Ilion will only be conquered by the race of Achilles."

"Would you dare to counsel cowardly flight?" roared Ajax. "Will the blood of our brother remain unavenged? Oh, perfidious individual, perhaps it was you, weary of combat and impatient for Penelope's couch, who wove the trap and pushed Achilles to death . . . if so, I'll have your life."

He launched himself forward menacingly.

Calmly, Ulysses declared: "It's necessary to send ships to Neoptolemus. The son will avenge the father and finish his work."

The venerable Nestor raised his arms: "O you, well-named the subtle, wisdom reigns in your words. Let us not throw ourselves into sterile struggles; the hour of reprisals will come when the young warrior of Scyros can fight with us. Inflate the sails with favorable winds, bring back to us the proud scion of the fallen oak, whose immense shadow protected us. And you, chief of kings, magnanimous Agamemnon, send a demand for the body of Achilles; Priam will render the hero who rendered Hector to him. Let us prepare august funeral rites and honor the manes of the greatest among us."

A rumor, vague at first, grew, like a distant wave rolling toward the shore; over the swell of laments roared the raucous appeal of buccinas; their lugubrious rhythmic cries exhaled desolation and fear.

On a litter borne by eight Ilian heralds, the body of the inanimate warrior appeared, in his armor, further magnified by rigid death. The convoy advanced all the way to the chiefs. The noble son of Anchises bowed before the assembly and his mouth opened.

"King of kings, Agamemnon, reflection on earth of great Jupiter, god of gods, the sublime Priam, my master, sends me to bring you the remains of the hero, whom he mourns with you . . ."

Violently, Ajax interrupted:

"Son of a viper, you are heavy with lies; feigned lamentations do not touch us; the tears in your eyes do not veil the joy in your heart."

"Chief," replied Aeneas, "my king's tears are sincere. Achilles rendered to him the son he had stolen from him; if he had lived, the hero would be, at this moment, the son of Priam, the husband of Polyxena."

"You lie!"

"Achilles emptied the cup of betrothal at the feast; he was receiving the princess from the hands of Hecuba tonight, in the temple of Apollo, when the anger of the god struck him."

"Your oath?"

"I swear it by the purity of the dawn that is illuminating us, by the Palladium, the sacred rampart of Ilion, and by the entrails of Venus, which bore me."

The Hellenes fell silent, heads bowed.

"Take the hero to his tent," ordered Agamemnon. "Let him repose under the guard of his men and let him be adorned for the funeral, over which the next sun will bleed."

Penthesilea, enfevered by waiting, stared at the pale dawn light filtered by the bays of the hut, diffusing its sadness over everything; her hearing strained toward the rumors, her expectation was enervated; Achilles had not returned.

The soul of the queen quivered with jealousy, but her pride dominated her dread. Would she inflict on the hero the insult of doubt, lowering herself to suspicion? Had she, finally, so little faith in her beauty?

She dared not admit her fears, and drove away her anguish, not wanting to tremble for the life of the beloved. What audacious individual would dare to attack the vanquisher of the proudest? When he departed he was so confident in his strength and the respect of his enemies! She neglected to think about the cowards.

The warrior woman's torment was aggravated by her silence. But to whom could she pour out her heart? Around her there were only the jealous slave and the Amazons, blasphemers of amour. And so much did the latter impose themselves on her weakness, so certain was Penthesilea of only finding scorn for her weakness in them, that she would have preferred to be alone with Briseis, to confide her terrors to her and weep together. At least the poor disdained woman knew how to love.

A tumult of footfalls hammered the ground, grew and fell silent before the threshold. A fist thumped the closed door.

Penthesilea leapt up; her muscular arm lifted the bar; under the rude pressure of the new arrivals the door gaped.

The warrior woman's hair stood on end; her beauty contracted in a mask of horror; the face of the Gorgon was impregnated in her convulsed features, her eyes bulging and her teeth menacing behind the rictus of twisted lips, and bloody sweat flowed heavily from her livid forehead.

On the same funeral bed her despair saw two cadavers: Atys and Achilles! For the second time, her love had given death.

Behind her, a plaint prolonged her dolor and a cry of triumph insulted it. The Amazons saluted with their hatred the death of their master and conqueror.

Penthesilea ran, menace in her mouth, her fist brandished, her eyes bloodshot, but she softened at Briseis' sobs. The queen turned to the slave, put her arms around her, and the two of them embraced, their souls sisterly, united in the same distress.

The Amazons fell silent, scornfully.

Penthesilea assaulted their harsh faces with her gaze. Her majesty tamed them; she was their queen; her gesture expelled them from the hall and the warrior women obeyed.

Alone with her sister in despair she stripped the hero of his armor, purified his body, anointed it with kisses and tears. She braided his beard and hair and drowned them in perfumes. Then she dressed the dead man in a light line tunic and a bright crimson robe.

Then, kneeling down without a word, the lover sank into a grim contemplation.

Stoically, she saw him carried away to the pyre, jealous of her mourning, the agony of which her pride wanted to hide from the cruelty of the Hellenes. But when the door was closed again, she felt that her soul had departed with Achilles and she prostrated herself on the ground.

When the flames had consumed the hero's remains, Ulysses and Ajax disputed the glory of bearing his weapons. The gilded tongue of the wily king of Ithaca prevailed over the valor of his rival.

Heralds knocked at the hut of Achilles. The door remained closed to their appeal. Then they proclaimed in a loud voice the judgment of the chiefs and demanded its execution.

Suddenly, the batten opened; a terror sprang forth therefrom; on the threshold, Achilles seemed to live again, standing in his armor.

Penthesilea had put on the golden helmet and the cnemides and buckled on the sword, had taken hold of the buckler and was leaning on the invincible lance.

Superbly, she declared: "Come and take them!"

Ulysses became irritated, brandishing the shaft of his lance in order to chastise the messengers with it, but prudence mastered his arm and his mouth alone delivered his anger.

"Cowards! Sons of dogs! Are you men who tremble before a woman?"

The first stammered: "I thought I was seeing Achilles again."

The second continued: "She incarnated Bellona."

"She is so beautiful," ventured the third.

Ulysses thought about it. "No matter," he affirmed, after a silence. "The chiefs of the army have awarded me Achilles' weapons; a woman, a captive, will not steal that honor from me. She will not vanquish where Ajax was vanquished. If force seemed reckless, my brain is fertile in ruses. Return to Penthesilea and announce to her humbly that Ulysses, moved by her misfortune, abandons the prize of valor to her, as the more worthy."

The queen believed in the chief's flattery. Ulysses then presented himself before her, respectful of his adversity, admiring her courage. She was obliged to offer her guest the cup of amity and drink with him.

Immediately, a heavy sleep overtook Penthesilea. When she awoke, the weapons had disappeared.

She raced to Ulysses' camp.

At dawn a ship had been taken from the shore by the matelots, and, balanced on the water, its sails were already inflated by winds that were blowing toward Scyros.

The Amazon perceived the triumphant traitor standing on the deck. Accompanied by the sons of the great Theseus, Acamas and Demophon, and by the aged Phoenix, whose cares had fortified the childhood of Achilles' heir, Ulysses was going on behalf of the chiefs of the army to demand from Neoptolemus the support of his arm.

The imprecations of Penthesilea troubled the camp and provoked the anger of the Atride. The Amazon and her companions were thrown, laden with chains, into the depths of the Myrmidon hulls to await their new master.

The outrage done to her majesty, the shame of being treated as a slave, and the haughty scorn of the Amazons blew into the heart of Penthesilea an incendiary hatred of the male.

The storm swept away the ashes accumulated over the former hearth by amour, and the reignited volcano seethed, ready to vomit its lava. Her sisters stimulated the fire, burning therein the relics of amour, exciting their queen to implacable revenge, to disgust for man, the cowardly slave of his flesh, a filthy pig wallowing in the material, tamed by a smile and dominated in his soul by inviolate woman.

Meanwhile, the young man born of the amours of Achilles and the blonde child Deidamia, cherished daughter of the king of Scyros, flattered by the divine oracle and being implored by the superb Atride, had come aboard Ulysses' ship and was riding the waves, impatient at the slowness of the winds that were delaying his glory.

Finally, the blue-tinted blur of the Trojan hills surged from the horizon, the solid mass of that Ilion promised to his arms, the host of masts hoisted by the ships, and then, on the plain, the camp populated by the swarming crowd of warriors. Neoptolemus' breast swelled for a cry of triumph, which was stifled by his lips. That land also contained the tomb of Achilles.

And more profoundly than the love of glory, vengeance entered his filial heart.

As soon as the watchmen had identified the hull illuminated with bright colors, the chiefs ordered the preparation of a great feast; but as soon as he had rendered his homage to Agamemnon, Neoptolemus refused to celebrate his arrival on the land of his mourning. Without resting, he headed toward the tumulus that crowned the promontory of Sigea with its mass.

He sacrificed a bull in order to obtain from Achilles the heritage of his strength, and chose a black one to satisfy the infernal gods; then, having spread the ritual libations over the pyre, he pronounced his oath.

"Achilles, my father, I swear to combat in your name and not to lay down my arms until the day when the last of your murderers has paid for your death with his life."

Gravely, he returned to the chiefs and demanded the paternal heritage.

"Neoptolemus," declared the Atride, "my heralds will guide you to your father's hut; you will receive the spoils acquired by his arm, the slaves captive in his hulls, everything that as his. Only the weapons forged by Vulcan . . ."

"My father's weapons!"

"They belong to the son of Laertes, by the vote of the army."

Neoptolemus protested. "What! You invoke the aid of my arm, and without my consent you deprive me of my most glorious heritage? And it is the man who came, full of gilded words, to beg me in your name, who possesses them? That is too insulting. Either the weapons are rendered to me, or within the hour I will take to the sea again, and Achilles' soldiers will depart with me."

"Young man," declared Ulysses, "your youth is presumptuous. Have you suffered with us? Have you exposed your breast to enemy darts? And you dare to dispute the trophy of glory with the hero of so many battles! I was preferred to Ajax. Can you compare yourself to him? When your arm has weighed upon conquered Ilion, I will recognize your rights and cede the heritage, then merited, to you."

Agamemnon extended his scepter.

"Let it be so!"

Neoptolemus withdrew, his soul hardened with anger by the sovereign decision of the Atride. He wanted to vanquish in order to reclaim the weapons forged by Vulcan and made illustrious by Achilles, and that ambition exasperated his thirst for glory.

On the open space that extended in front of the hut of Achilles, Automedon presented the horses and chariots to his new chief. Then the guards brought forth the captives.

They filed past arrogantly before the gaze of the master. At the sight of the beautiful Harmothoa the young man was moved; he designated her with a gesture.

"For my bed."

The Amazon had heard; her face remained impassive. She raised her fists. A slack rope united them; she knotted it around her neck and spread her arms. Her face turned violet, the tumefied tongue protruded from her mouth and Harmothoa fell, stiffening her murderous hands until she was dead.

Neoptolemus recoiled; the stupor of his gaze interrogated the warrior women.

"Such we are; we can only conceive freely; to the caresses of a master we prefer death."

The Amazons shivered at Penthesilea's speech; they had found their queen again.

Strong in the courage of her companions, the princess extolled the rites of her people.

"We scorn amour! The male is merely the propagator of the race; freely we accept him, and reject him when his work is accomplished; we remain the sole mistresses of the fruit of our wombs. Thus, we only give birth to free beings. Seek your pleasures with the cowardly daughters of our homeland; before being yours, every one of us will be dead."

The flame radiated by her eyes burned Neoptolemus; subjugated by her savage speech and ecstasized by her splendor, he asked: "Free, would you love me?"

She looked at the young man; Achilles was reflected in his son, but her warriors were there and her heart had hardened under its bruises. She smiled disdainfully.

"Amour only enters into cowardly hearts."

"You were my father's!"

"Son unworthy of him, you insult me! Achilles respected me."

Neoptolemus became irritated. "I am your master; your body belongs to me . . ."

"When my soul has quit it."

The young man became absorbed and taciturn. All force would break against that will; all violence would be fatal. His desire possessed him, already too powerful for him to renounce its satisfaction. He would wait, then. The slow hours of captivity would depress the will and humble the splendid Amazon. Then she would be pliant to his wishes, and perhaps would offer herself to his kiss of her own accord . . .

"Let the prisoners be locked up," he ordered.

He entered under his roof, and his solitary evening confronted him with two struggles undertaken for two conquests: the weapons of Achilles and the seduction of Penthesilea; that of glory and that of amour. And his large heart beat more forcefully.

IX
Neoptolemus

NEOPTOLEMUS appeared in the plain, and Paris succumbed against the son, just as Hector had fallen under the arm of the father. His vengeance unslaked, he rushed to battle like a lion to carnage. He was in haste to break through the wall and to immolate on the tumulus of Achilles that Polyxena whose deceptive amour had precipitated the death of the hero; finally, the mere sight of Ulysses, clad in the divine armor, made his blood boil.

Thus, when Priam's son Helenus, the illustrious diviner, was captured by Ulysses, and revealed to the Greeks that Pergame would only fall under the arrows of Hercules. Neoptolemus joined the king of Ithaca to go to Philoctetes, the possessor of those arrows, to obtain from the son of Poeas the pardon of the Hellenes, who had abandoned him on the isle of Lemnos, weary of the plaints that a horrible wound extracted from the hero. In spite of his rancor, Philoctetes allowed himself to be persuaded by the son of Achilles, and they both became irritated by the excessively slow realization of the oracles.

A prisoner, Penthesilea fortified herself in the hatred of men, proud of having merited the respect and admiration of her companions. The Amazons stimulated the resistance of their queen by deference and speech. All of them, in her presence, competed in proofs of devotion and signs of veneration. They exalted the grandeur of her soul, and it was pleasant for the captive to feel that she was a queen again.

Yes, she was a worthy daughter of the god of battles, the incomparable heroine of the race. So the temptation of a new amour could not make inroads into her heart, vain in her reconquered prestige and inflamed by the ardor that her warriors stimulated in her.

Ilion fell. Neoptolemus recovered the weapons of Achilles, without Penthesilea being vanquished.

And the hero, unsatisfied by the glory, set sail, taking his captives and his booty, his head bowed like a fallen man. One sole ambition possessed him; for him, only one triumph existed: the love of a slave!

Even the passive submission of Penthesilea to his desire would not have satisfied his heart. He had wanted her for her beauty; now he loved her for her resistance and her grandeur.

Penthesilea, leaning over the wake, watched the waves flee, and the sea, as it extended, magnified her exile. Neoptolemus admired her proud forehead, which rebelled against dolor.

"Woman, would you like half my kingdom?"

Disdainfully, the Amazon replied: "Your father offered me its entirety."

"What do you want, then?"

"Liberty."

"As queen you would be free."

"No, I would belong to a king."

"He would be at your feet"

"He would get up again as my master."

"Do you not see my amour, then?"

"What does it matter to me?"

Chagrin hollowed out a wrinkle in the pure forehead of the beautiful warrior woman.

"All women would be proud to be loved by the son of Achilles and the conqueror of Ilion."

"Love them."

"You alone possess my heart."

"I return it to you."

"How far, in order to attain you, is it necessary to elevate my passion and my glory?"

"The heart of an Amazon is too high for amour."

"You will love me!"

"Abandon the hope."

"Remember that I am begging you, and that I could constrain you."

She suspended herself over the water. "Dare!"

"Have no fear!" he cried, alarmed. "I only want you of your own will."

She smiled pityingly.

"See what amour makes of a brave man! And you want me to be cowardly enough to love? I only have the soul of a warrior."

Heavy clouds stained the horizon, as stormy as the hero's heart. The sails flapped, tormented by gusts, the sea swelled its waves; multiplied in a torrential surge, as tumultuous as the collision of battle, they rushed, collapsed, reared up again, drooling like the mouths of hydras, and twisted like rabid dogs avid to bite.

Neoptolemus was constrained to flee before the tempest. Lemnos, from which he had extracted Philoctetes, served as a refuge. At night, in the cavern populated by the memory of the great exile, he hoped in vain for the peace of slumber. Penthesilea's refusal obsessed his insomnia. The grim warrior woman! How much more lovable her pride made her to his heart! In his soldierly ambition, amour impassioned him for combat and victory.

A suspicion insinuated itself into the thought of the master and grew. Isolation might tame the princess and render her exorable to words of love. In the midst of her savage Amazons, she retempered her resistance in their exhortations and their example. Solitary, the long hours would enlarge her brain, populating it with dreams; the need for confidences and tenderness would erode that displaced soul, and through the breach one might be able to penetrate into her and emerge victorious.

At daybreak the sea had calmed down and the flotilla set sail again. Penthesilea did not find her companions, embarked on another vessel by the king's order. She sensed the trap and became indignant, but her scorn dominated her anger; she remained arrogant, and did not deign to complain.

Prouder in her bearing, more indifferent in her gaze and haughtier in her smile, she stood up to the master, who spied on her. Her indomitable will hardened her soul. A slave, she sustained her strength and remained queen. Neoptolemus' words collided with absolute silence. Penthesilea did not seem to see or hear him, her eyes looking upwards and her ears closed to the sounds of the earth.

Passion burned the hero, bruising his eyelids with insomnia and scaling his lips with fever. He agitated like a captive beast in the narrow prison in which his ship held him. Contrary winds drove the flotilla away from the Malian coasts, and Neoptolemus felt himself consumed by the contact of the woman who, his by right of war, defied him and whom he dared not force to his desire, the vanquished woman whose majesty dominated him.

He became indignant at his weakness and swore to act as a master, but the mere sight of Penthesilea subjugated him, and his brutal frenzy foundered in admiration.

Glorying at first in the harm caused by her empire, Penthesilea soon felt her loins stirring. Pity was born in her for the bold warrior, the young man, so handsome, who was ravaged by her rigor. She scolded herself for such compassion toward an enemy, but that enemy was now her victim, wounded by her . . . and her heart remembered the caress of Achilles. Then she became afraid of loving again!

She cursed the cowardice of her sex. Her isolation terrified her; her strength was all in her companions.

Ah, rather than fall again, she would chastise her tyrannical flesh with death and finally liberate herself! And, magnified by the sacrifice made to her glory, she smiled at the sea and threw herself into it.

The water opened hospitably and received her in its shelter.

Already, with a bold arm, Nepotolemus was attacking the waves, striving to penetrate their homicidal eddies. The abyss guarded the refugee in its arcana. The hero exhausted himself in struggles, resolved to unite himself with his beloved in her tomb rather than abandon her to death.

Thetis learned of the peril of her son's son; she lifted the body of Penthesilea to the surface of the water. Neopotolemus took possession of it and climbed aboard his ship with the inanimate Amazon.

Penthesilea opened her eyes. With a surly gesture she pushed away the warrior leaning over her face, who was contemplating her, glorying in having saved her, his soul filled with faith in her gratitude. Only these words broke the Amazon's mutism:

"My sisters?"

Neoptolemus knelt down.

"Do you finally believe in my love, princess? It has conquered you from death."

She turned her eyes away and repeated: "My sisters?"

That indifference crushed the hero. He abandoned all hope.

"Your will shall be done."

He gave the order to accost the vessel containing the Amazon. Penthesilea was transported aboard it. Neoptolemus was unable to resolve to remain in the presence of the woman who refused his desperate love.

The welcome of her companions reinforced the weakening soul of the young queen. The last appeal of the hero had almost vanquished her; the effort required for the refusal had revealed to her that she would not have had the energy to resist a further invocation. She had even had to hide her gaze in order not to betray herself.

However, she did not love Neoptolemus; he appeared to her eyes as the reflection of the happiness for which she had hoped with Achilles and had known in the arms of Atys.

The awakening had quivered in her intimate fibers, and her being, weaned from the joys savored, was exasperated by her desire. No, she did not love Neoptolemus, but she would have liked to gasp under his kiss.

Surrounded by her proud Amazons, she hoped to be invulnerable in them as in armor. She would be strong in the impassivity of their flesh and the power of their hatred. Among them, the lover of the dream foundered in male disgrace.

Neoptolemus could not suspect that he had been so close to triumph, and his ulcerated heart was lost in the disarray of defeat.

Suddenly, he experienced the need to act as a master, to belie his past by means of excesses, to avenge his weakness by brutality. The man ceded to the tyrant. On his order wines were brought; he drank himself breathless. When drunk, he had his Trojan captives appear before him. Then, without regard for the tears of his victims, at the hazard of the madness of his bestial frenzy, without desire, he soiled virgins in front of their mothers, and mothers in front of their children.

Then he prostrated himself in the brutishness of his ignominy.

He wanted to forget, and, depressed by woman, his soul of a hero degraded itself in the orgy.

X

FINALLY, the Malian shore hoisted its mountainous soil over the watery plain, dominated in the distance by the mass of the formidable Oeta, the pedestal that had been required for the pyre of Hercules. The warriors saluted the fatherland with an acclamation that concluded in melancholy. Over the joy of rediscovering the natal hearth floated the anxiety of mourning. Would everyone find the mother, the wife and the children deserted ten years ago? Would wives recognize their husbands in these men worn away by combats and ravaged by wounds? Would they rediscover in the aged wives, dried up by widowhood, the blonde vision carried away by their eyes and retained in memory?

The captives curbed their shoulders before the land of slavery, and the fatherland, the ancestral fields that they would never see again, seemed more distant. They would labor heavily under the yoke of a master, cultivating foreign soil, weary and somber, without relieving their labor with the healthy contentment with which labor recompenses the free man.

With mute, impassive faces the Amazons saw the land.

The approach of the vessels assembled the river-dwelling population on the strand. Women, old men and children huddled expectantly, dreaming about husbands, sons and fathers . . .

Finally, the hulls bit the sand, were engraved and came to a halt. The warriors, after ten years of absence, trod the paternal soil with their feet.

The sadness of belated returns! The woman hesitated before the mutilated man; the warrior refused to rediscover the bride, the lover of spring nights, in the matron; and the majority of the fathers were dead. Each man, returned to his old dwelling, sat down, bleak and weary, beside the fire that he had lit in is youth, and whose cold ashes no longer warmed his heart and his lame limbs.

They resumed the old occupations, but their hands had forgotten the manipulation of the hoe and the plow; even the earth seemed ingrate to them.

And on returning to their abode, worn out by the war, overwhelmed by fatigue, they found their wives too old to give them sons.

They regretted the sack of Ilion and the beautiful young women known on the steps of the temples, victims that death kept eternally young in their memory.

※

Parked separately, on the royal lands, the Amazons endured their exile. Then, an incurable ennui weighed upon them. Their past captivity had been filled by the events of the war, had known the anxious expectation of combats, had been animated by joys and angers agitated in them by the reverses and successes of their masters. After the ruination of Ilion, the peripeties of the sea journey had occupied their eyes. Henceforth, they were entangled in the monotony of days without emotion and without hope. The tomb held their life!

The great hearts of the Amazons bled for the extinct posterity, but tamed the tyranny of the flesh by means of a higher will.

Nature, on the other hand, avenged her scorned rights. Bitter blood burned their bodies. Fever rendered their limbs fleshless and, far from softening, the Amazons were exasperated by hatred of their master, and by the fury of their captivity, the source of their woes.

They remained proud, grouped around their queen like a guard of honor, and secretly forming a rampart against the past weakness, a return of which they feared; their own struggles revealed to them the strength of the danger. The five survivors of the sacred squadron—the blonde Clonie; Autandre, the expert in training bloodhounds; Evadre, the tamer of restive stallions; Polemusa, the singer of hymns of war; and Thermodusa, the best wielder of the lance—still watched over the honor of the condemned race.

Moons had succeeded moons, seasons had succeeded seasons, and for the second time, the year by the year, without eroding the resistance of the captives. In vain, liberty had been offered to those who would accept a husband; they were immured in a disdainful silence.

Spectrally, the warriors wandered in the enclosure that held them prisoner. The blonde Clonie was no more!

Impotent, the daughter of Mars still felt herself perennially bound by the laws of her people. But outraged Amour took his revenge. The neglect of his worship undermined the atheists, and ravaged the imprudent rebels with his immortal laws. The deniers of sentiment, who had never sacrificed except to the act, expired of distress in their isolation; vengeful Amour, before throwing them to death, devoured their beauty in a sinister fashion.

The Amazons were mortified by the stigmata with which a premature decrepitude withered their atrophied youth. They were, from then on, the sterile tree that the ax will fell.

And the ax struck. The daughter of the ardent gallops, Evadre, was the next to fall, stricken under the yoke. The blood flowing to her brain burst her veins and engulfed her thought, and like an oak struck by lightning, in the carbonized face of death, her anger still sweated.

Polemusa, Autandre and Thermodusa were frightened by the horrific mask that their sister wore with the somber seal of accursed races. However, they adorned her body for the funeral and carried her to the pyre.

Penthesilea remained impenetrable while the Amazons testified their dolor irresistibly;

the departure of each of them shrank their fatherland.

Soon, the singing of hymns of war no longer breathed its heroism into the hours of long evenings; only the waves of the Sperchius, which swells the Achelous with its torrential waters, sobbed over the banks. Polemusa lost the vibrant voice that exalted their hearts to greater courage. She no longer retold the exploits of the ancestors, she no longer sustained her companions with the remembrance of great examples. She languished, her eyes extinct and her lips discolored; a hoarse cough racked her throat and its swell bobbed a flaccid nipple on her breast; a shadow accumulated on her pale forehead; the last drops of blood overflowed her mouth and their leakage carried her life away.

Before the new cadaver the proud warriors knew tears for the first time; Autandre and Thermodusa hugged one another recklessly, as if to be stronger against death together.

Only Penthesilea remained dry-eyed.

From then on, anguish oppressed the heart of Autandre. Specters haunted her nights, enfevering her with terrors, drowning her face in cold sweats. Breathless, the warrior woman, once so valorous, frightened by rumors, veiled her head, as fearful and weak as a child. In vain, Thermodusa hugged her to her untamed breast, cradled her with soft words and pampered her with caresses; Autandre writhed in her arms, delirious, crying in agony, to stiffen, inanimate. Her companion bathed her temples, breathing life into her mouth to mouth, but only reawakened in her an uncertain, vacillating flame ready to go out.

The soul of Thermodusa, previously impervious to pity, became maternal. She disputed her sister with death like an only child. The haughty indifference of Penthesilea, faithful in its hardness to the pride of her race, appeared monstrous to Thermodusa. Once, she had envied that character of impassivity; in the distress of her imminent abandonment she judged it odious and criminal. She shivered at the thought of living alone in the company of that pitiless queen when Autandre was gone!

Her despair was indurated with hatred and horror. Every crisis that pushed Autandre toward the tomb rendered the dying woman dearer to Thermodusa and increased her resentment against the ferocious Penthesilea. So, when her lips, in kissing her companions, encountered the cold rigidity of death, the breath of life expired in them.

✳

Thermodusa reposes, dead, next to the dead woman she loved. Leaning over the bodies of her last two companions, Penthesilea straightens up, her face radiant with a savage joy.

And these words dilate her breast:

"Free at last!"

XI
Penthesilea

"DRINK!" cried Neoptolemus.

The gesture, which threw him back on to the bed, upset the cup.

The silver rang on the paving stones and its limpid voice prolonged the pure vibrations over the racket of mastications, words and laughter.

A tempest of clamors, an interminable echo, inflated the king's cry.

"Drink . . . ! Drink . . . !"

Drunkenness already inflamed the sweaty faces, parting slovenly robes over breasts, thickening tongues, and floated, troubled, in eyes. Raised heads fell back on to cushions heavily, and the courtesans, in order to awaken desire, their girdles unfastened and their tunics agape, displayed their beauties.

The servants brought leather bottles.

"Do you take me for a Phrygian slave?" yelped Neoptolemus, splashing the contents of his cup in the face of the cup-bearer. "Your wine stinks of he-goat, like the hair in your armpits. I want the gilded liquor that my divine ancestor sent me in jars from Scyros. Let's throw out the slaves, unworthy of that sacred wine! The women will serve us drink!"

A new acclamation burst forth amid the enthusiastic stamping of feet, the clinking of vessels and the thumping of fists on the tables.

All clamored: "The women! The women!"

Slowly, they got up, without readjusting their robes or their loose hair. They took possession of the amphorae, inclined them over their arms, and went round filling the cups. Their gestures, sometimes uncertain, let the odorous wine cascade in streams, the golden droplets of which constellated the pink marble of their bare feet.

As they passed by, the men drew them closer, snuffling the roses of their mouths with kisses and marking their delicate flesh with rude caresses. Laughter inflated the necks of the hetaerae like cooing doves, and the flowers of their nipples scintillated under the swell of breasts like the glints that sunlight extracts from the polished points of shields.

Crouching on fleeces at his feet, Neoptolemus had kept the blonde Chrysothemis and Oeonone with the hair darker that the plumage of a crow. Those two young women shared his favors, for the king had already wearied of the bed of Hector's widow, Andromache, in whose arms he had attempted to deceive the passion rejected by Penthesilea. The two favorites were attentive rivals, anxious to attract the preference of the master.

Penthesilea came in.

She had painted her eyebrows, cheeks and lips, and crowned her forehead with roses; a veil woven from light clouded her with its vaporous weave. A heavy crimson mantle embroidered with large golden lilies broadened her figure and undulated in her wake; it opened over a hyacinth robe florid with luminous gems. Precious necklaces were stacked over her throat and the bracelets on her arms awoke a clink of gold in the hieratic gesture that held them vertical.

She slid slowly toward the royal bed. Silence fell upon the orgy. Finally, she reached Neoptolemus and, standing up, held him under her gaze.

"What do you want?"

She tamed him with her last pride.

"You!"

The king contemplated her, a smile on his lips. His brutal hand parted the veil, lifted up the necklaces, touched the flesh. Then he fell back upon the cushions and his laughter burst forth formidably.

A worse outrage stung the Amazon; the hetaerae insulted her with their disdainful sniggers. She straightened up and said:

"Do you want me?"

"To the pigs!" hiccupped Neoptolemus, in is insulting gaiety. "Someone throw this painted idol out!"

Penthesilea plunged into the night. She went straight ahead, scaling crests, crossing torrents, forcing through woods, scattering the shreds of her sumptuous veils to the brambles. She went further and higher, incessantly, careless of precipices, insensible to the rocks stigmatized by the imprint of her bloody feet, pursued by jeers. The fire of her shame seemed to tear a flamboyant hole in the density of the darkness and she fled, seeking the desert, the lair of wild beasts, the inaccessible aerie of eagles.

She climbed, climbed higher, hoisted herself up from ledge to edge toward the inviolate summits. The plaint of nocturnal birds sobbed her shame; their fluttering flight slapped her face. Increasing haste precipitated her retreat, carrying her higher, ever higher, and as she attained the summit, the shelter of which she had hoped to conquer, as a supreme insult, on the horizon, a pale radiance magnified a laugh.

She stopped, desperate.

The dawn broke, white under the low sky. Daylight unfurled, lividly, in heavy waves of somber clouds. A yellow light stained the atmosphere. A torpor crushed the earth with a stifling lid.

There was not a breath in the bleak silence: everywhere, desolation and death.

Penthesilea raised herself up to her full height on the culminating summit. Beneath her gaped an extinct crater filled by the rain. The water, as smooth as a mirror, reflected the queen.

Her eyes, weary of reflecting an inclement sky, lowered. The pitiless lake sent her image back to the woman. She closed her eyes in terror of seeing.

A gust of wind passed over her forehead, and a bird of prey flew over, hectically, sowing the snigger of its hoarse cry. Oh, that laughter! The laughter with which her vanquisher had insulted her! She could still hear it; she would hear it forever. The humiliation of offering herself had not been sufficient; she had had to suffer the outrage of being scorned. She, the beauty of beauties, on the sublime forehead of whom Achilles had placed his diadem, into whose hand he had put his heart! And the insult came to her from Neoptolemus, who had conquered the sea for her!

Was that the revenge for the ancient disdain with which she had contemplated his amour? A coward, to avenge himself thus! A coward, who mocked her without decency before the lubricity of guests and the livestock of courtesans!

And like the king, they had all laughed. The splendor of her flesh had not dazzled them; not one gaze had been illuminated by a glint of desire. Doubt bit into her pride. Oh, this was too much suffering. She would have the courage to know.

She opened her eyes, but before plunging into contemplation of herself she gazed into space again.

Immense rays springing from the sun, buried under the mass of clouds, were elongated like the fulgurant blades of swords of light. The light of a forge in darkness, red and bloody . . .

The air was hot, charged with tempests; a great silence oppressed nature; everything was overwhelmed by the menace of imminent wrath clamored by thunder.

New clouds surged forth; the last gaze of the sky was extinguished, like the gleam of pupils behind falling eyelids; a leaden shroud tightened about the shrunken horizon, weighing upon mute, inert things gathered in a fearful flock.

Penthesilea removed the last diadem from her head, a withered crown that her angry fingers crumpled, and then, sadly, scattered the roses.

The veil flowed away; she released the clasp of the mantle that spread out behind her in heavy waves, red with the blood of her heart.

Her hands trembled over the knot of her belt, the knot that she had hoped to see broken by the beloved, and which his disdain had not even brushed. It ran in loose pleats and coiled like a snake at her feet.

The robe slid from her shoulders; a final modesty brightened her pallor, but with a bitter, grim resolution she tore away the chlamys.

With the cast of her rings and necklaces she troubled the water in order not to see yet . . . and beneath the wrath of the sky, she stood up, naked . . .

The sheet was wrinkled by orbicular frissons that blurred the images. Gradually, Penthesilea perceived more distinct reflections; finally, absolute calm descended.

Then she saw.

Wildly, she turned her gaze in order to recognize the phantom that had substituted itself for her.

She was alone. Leaning over the water, however, she had seen an unknown form reflected: a frightful skeleton. The legs, whose thin tibias were knotted by bony knees and fleshless thighs, supported a flaccid belly striped by earthy furrows; an empty teat hung over a withered breast; ruts sank between sharp ribs; profound recesses accentuated the projection of bones and angular shoulders from which formless arms jutted like the tentacles of a squid. The neck twisted its rope of meager tendons, from which slack skin hung, The face, stretched by horror, was cut by a mouth with lips so pale that they seemed absent; only the eyes were alive, blazing in the center of bruised, crumpled, sanguinary eyelids, and over the leaden forehead, scaled with black cracks, the hair bristled with the forked tongues of Medusa's vipers.

She looked again.

The same specter was imposed on her contemplation.

Alone . . . she was alone.

With a supreme energy she bent her head and ran her irreparable gaze over the same nudity.

Then she understood.

She understood the error of her life and the malediction that had blasted her in her pride.

Disfigured irredeemably, she penetrated the eternal laws. She understood the rights of the double being, man and woman, their union, the sanctity of the family, its grandeur, its consolatory duties, the power of its bond; the woman wife and mother, the man protector and chief . . .

The rites of her race terrified her by virtue of their atrocity and mendacity.

To live, oh, to live a new existence of submission and amour! Her error bore its own punishment within it. But could she not hope? Was she not still young? No, she was old, desiccated, withered . . . Her fist bruised her sterile womb, her empty teat . . . The sap had dried up.

The truth had been illuminated too late.

A revolt raised her head and twisted her mouth to blaspheme the gods . . . The thunder threw back the anathema.

She was accursed.

One last time, she contemplated the reflection of her image in the abyss, and, her eyes crazed and her teeth parted to bite, she hurled herself into it.

The gulf swallowed her.

The ripples died way; mute and heavy, the water no longer reflected anything but the bleak impassivity of the heavens.